REA

ACPL
DISCARDED

ALLEN COUNTY PUBLIC LIBRARY

W9-CSX-244

MAY 1 9 2000

Lover
and Deceiver

***Other Five Star Titles
by Cathie Linz:***

Pride and Joy

Lover and Deceiver

Cathie Linz

Five Star
Unity, Maine

Copyright © 1986 by Cathie Linz

All rights reserved.

Five Star Romance Series
Published in 2000 in conjunction with Cathie Linz

Cover photograph © Alan J. La Vallee.

The text of this edition is unabridged.

Set in 11 pt. Plantin by Al Chase.

Printed in the United States on permanent paper.

Library of Congress Cataloging-in-Publication Data
Linz, Cathie.
  Lover and deceiver / Cathie Linz.
    p.   cm.
  ISBN 0-7862-2369-3 (hc : alk. paper)
  1. Community theater—Fiction. I. Title.
PS3562.I558 L6 2000
813'.54—dc21   99-086900

ACKNOWLEDGMENTS

Many thanks to the Village Theatre Guild for allowing me to sit in on their rehearsal and to Sue K. in particular for patiently answering my many questions.

Thanks also to Pam Morris and the people at the Portland Convention and Visitors' Center, for supplying me with so much information about their lovely city.

And special thanks to Marilyn for buying a brass bed on the layaway plan! Rabbit, rabbit, rabbit, Marilyn!

CHAPTER ONE

"I want to speak to someone in charge!" a male voice demanded. *"Now!"*

Erin Rossi lowered the play she was reading and peered over the top of the pages to briefly study the man who'd made the seething announcement. His authoritative appearance matched his voice.

He didn't look like the usual customer who came into Courtesy Dry Cleaners. For one thing, he was too formally dressed. It was Saturday morning, yet he was decked out in a three-piece suit, vest and all! He was very tall, well over six feet. The dark color of his suit emphasized his height. His dark hair was conservatively styled, and he wore dark-rimmed glasses that reminded her of Clark Kent's and concealed the color of his eyes. But nothing concealed the impatient anger of his expression.

Bracing herself for trouble, Erin sighed in frustration and lowered her book back to the desk. At this rate she'd never finish reviewing the first act, let alone the entire play. As the director of the upcoming community theater production, Erin had to have the script firmly fixed in her mind by the time auditions began in two days. While she'd already read the play through numerous times, she wanted to examine it again for specific details of characterization and pacing.

With that thought in mind, Erin had planned on spending her Saturday lying on a chaise lounge in her front yard, soaking up the lovely August sun and preparing for Monday evening's auditions, undisturbed by interruptions. But even the best-laid plans had a way of going astray.

Case in point—Erin's sister Mary hadn't *planned* on having her baby for another month yet. But Mary had gone into premature labor early this morning, exactly half an hour after her husband had flown from Portland, Oregon's International Airport to the East Coast for a two-day business seminar. Luckily, for all concerned, Erin's parents lived nearby and were able to take Mary to the hospital. While Erin's parents were taking care of Mary, Erin was taking care of her parents' dry cleaning business.

Rising to her feet, Erin tucked a lock of her shoulder-length hair behind one ear. Her hairstyle's asymmetrical part and blunt cut gave her the look of a dark-haired Greta Garbo. Unfortunately the baggy blue smock she wore was more reminiscent of Harpo Marx. The smock, which bore the logo of Courtesy Cleaners and belonged to her mother, was several sizes too large, but it was the only smock Erin had been able to locate. Despite that handicap, she still managed to summon a smile as she approached the angry-looking man. "May I help you?"

"I doubt it," he retorted with a dismissive look that really aggravated Erin. "I want to speak to someone in charge."

"So you've already said. Quite loudly, as a matter of fact." Erin strove to keep her own voice calm, but it was not easy. Restraint had never been her strong point, not with her combined Irish and Italian background.

The man, unaware of Erin's volatile nature, continued to push his luck by delivering a sarcastic sermon. "Perhaps if you paid attention instead of reading on the job, a customer wouldn't have to yell to gain your attention."

Erin's expression darkened ominously. Those who knew her would have recognized the danger signs in her hazel eyes and sought shelter from the imminent storm of her temper.

The effort of banking her anger made her reply brief. "You've gained my attention."

"Are you in charge here?"

She answered his question as arrogantly as he'd asked it. "For the time being."

"I've got a serious complaint."

"Really?" Erin did not appear at all intimidated. "What seems to be the problem?"

He took the plastic-covered clothes he was holding and tossed them onto the counter. "These aren't mine."

"Oh? Whose are they, then?" she calmly asked.

"I don't know," he retorted. "And I don't care."

"I see."

"Do you?" The man glared at her. "I doubt that. I had a very important function to attend last night, and I had to do so without the trousers to my suit!"

"That must have caused quite a stir," Erin murmured with a commiserating shake of her head. She met his quelling stare without batting an eye. "Sorry." Her grin told him she was far from regretful. Normally she wouldn't have given one of her parents' customers such a hard time, but this man rubbed her the wrong way. "You were saying?"

"I want to know what you've done with my clothes!"

I pawned them. The words were on the tip of her tongue, and it took all of Erin's self-control to make sure they stayed there. Her parents had entrusted the business to her for the day, and that responsibility did not include alienating customers. Experience had already shown that this man did not appreciate her sense of humor, so she'd try to be polite. "I'm sorry for the mix-up. If you'll give me your name . . ."

"Garrett. Jonathan Garrett."

Erin turned to the serpentine line of hanging clothes and checked through all the orders beginning with G. No Garrett.

Of course not. That would be too easy.

"I don't suppose you still have your claim stub?" she asked hopefully.

"I handed it in when I picked up this order," Jonathan stated, as if that were a self-evident fact.

His arrogant inflection revoked Erin's intention of staying calm and courteous. "You didn't notice *then* that the order wasn't yours?"

"My suit jacket was on the top. I didn't think to go through every single item to make sure everything was mine. Obviously I should have. It would have saved me the shock of finding this"—Jonathan glared at a green-and-yellow-checked sport jacket clearly visible through the plastic—"in my closet!"

Erin was impressed. "I'll bet it glows in the dark!"

"This is no laughing matter."

Erin deliberately wiped the grin from her face and attempted to nod somberly. "I can see why you feel that way." The man obviously had no sense of humor, she decided as she removed the plastic from the loud jacket and went through the rest of the order. "None of these articles of clothing belong to you, is that correct?" As she voiced her question she held up a particularly frilly pair of silk baby-doll pajamas in hot pink.

Jonathan unclenched his teeth long enough to utter two curt words. "That's correct."

"Mmmm, I suppose pink isn't really your color," she decided, lowering the feminine nightwear to the counter.

Jonathan stood in stony silence as Erin checked the receipt still stapled to the plastic.

"Well?" Jonathan finally demanded.

"Well, what?" she countered while frowning at the receipt. The writing was her father's and therefore hard to decipher, which was why her mother normally wrote out the receipts. But then, things hadn't exactly been normal lately.

As if to prove that point, the phone rang just as Jonathan Garrett began another soliloquy of complaints. He stopped mid-word as Erin positively dived for the phone on the first ring.

"Courtesy Cleaners." Erin's face lit up with delight. "It is! She is! That's fantastic!" Pleased with the entire world, she impetuously cupped the receiver with her hand and joyfully told Jonathan, "It's a girl!"

"Who are you talking to?" Mrs. Rossi asked Erin.

"A customer, Mom."

"Is everything all right at the store?"

Erin voiced a hurried reassurance. "Fine. No problems. You're sure Mary's okay?"

"She's fine. Tired, of course, but quite pleased with herself."

"How's it feel to be a grandmother?" Erin asked in a teasing voice.

Her mother's reply was enthusiastic. "Wonderful! But what about your customers, Erin? Don't keep them waiting."

Erin rosily dismissed Jonathan's impatience. "There's only one customer, Mom, and he doesn't mind waiting."

"I mind waiting!" Jonathan practically roared.

"What was that?" her mother asked in a worried voice.

"Nothing, Mom. Just a bus backfiring." Erin glared at Jonathan for daring to interrupt her conversation. "Everything's under control here," she quickly reassured her mother. "Give Mary my love, and tell her I'll stop by the hospital tonight."

"Did you have to bellow like that?" she angrily demanded of Jonathan the moment she hung up the phone. "My sister just gave birth to a six-pound-ten-ounce baby girl."

"So?"

"So, you interrupted the entire thing!"

"I doubt that very much," Jonathan retorted in what might almost have been a wryly humorous tone were it not for the underlying thread of impatience running through his voice. "Now, about my missing order . . ."

Erin was angry enough to tell Jonathan Garrett exactly what he could do with his missing order!

Sensing her imminent outburst, Jonathan held up his hand in a gesture of supremacy. "Look, you can renew the family chronicles after I've left. Meanwhile, I do have an appointment this evening, and I'd like to get out of this dry cleaners with my order before then."

Erin's glare could have disintegrated solid steel as she gave Jonathan the evil eye. In contrast to her violent expression, her voice was syrupy-sweet when she spoke. "Rest assured, Mr. Garrett, that I'll do everything in my power to make sure you're out of here as soon as possible."

"I'm so relieved to hear that."

Erin didn't bother answering him. Instead she took the receipt she'd previously been studying and acted on a hunch. Her father's handwritten capital *G*'s bore a strong resemblance to a capital *S*, so perhaps the rest of Jonathan Garrett's order could be found in the *S* section.

Sure enough, there was an order under "Sarrett," and the clothing was unquestionably male. The dark, somber colors led her to believe that they did indeed belong to Mr. Garrett.

"Do these look familiar to you?" she asked Jonathan after laying the order across the counter.

"Very."

"Good. But we want to make sure there's no mistake this time. So let's see . . ." Erin held up each article of clothing and took great pleasure in itemizing them separately. "One pair of men's trousers, dark blue, very conservative-looking. Yours?"

"Mine."

"One conservatively cut, somber suit jacket, also dark blue. Yours?"

"Mine."

"Another pair of trousers, in somber black this time. Hold on! This pair appears to have pinstripes." Erin studied the material closely. "But maybe that's just a trick of the lights in here."

"You can cut the editorializing." Anger was evident in his curt demand.

Erin's hazel eyes widened with feigned innocence. "I'm just doing my job, Mr. Garrett. I wouldn't want you to be shocked again by any outrageous clothing that might be hidden in this order."

Jonathan's jaw was taut with self-restraint as he spoke in a gritty voice. "The clothes are all mine."

"Fine, If you'll just sign here . . ." Erin pointed to the line at the bottom of the Sarrett receipt.

"You're lucky I'm not demanding restitution," Jonathan informed her as he pulled an expensive-looking pen from the inner pocket of his jacket.

"Are you a lawyer?" Erin asked.

"Yes."

She nodded knowingly. "Figures."

Jonathan paused in the middle of writing his last name on the receipt. "What do you mean by that?"

"You look like a lawyer." Her observation was not meant to be a compliment, and it wasn't delivered as one.

Jonathan's smile was mocking. "I'm so glad you think so." He finished signing his name and carefully returned his pen to his jacket's inner pocket. He then deliberately allowed his eyes to linger over the baggy blue smock she was wearing. "You look like you should be doing what you do too."

So it was war, was it? she silently fumed. *Fine!* She knew exactly what battle tactics to use. Erin waited until Jonathan had gathered up his order and almost reached the door before firing her final salvo. "I hope you'll come back to Courtesy Cleaners the next time you lose your pants, Mr. Garrett!" She spoke the words loudly enough so that the group of customers who'd just walked in could hear her.

Jonathan froze for a moment before pivoting to face Erin. "The next time I lose my pants, you can be sure I'll come looking for you," he said in a drawl. A moment later he was gone.

CHAPTER TWO

Why did you let her get to you? Jonathan demanded of himself as he ferociously rammed the ball against the wall during his practice racquetball warm-up. Here it was Sunday afternoon and he was still brooding over what had happened at the dry cleaners yesterday.

Pausing to wipe the sweat from his forehead, Jonathan tried to pinpoint precisely what had upset him so much. The mix-up with his clothes had been damn inconvenient to be sure. And the young woman's attitude had been irreverently unconcerned. But what had really irked him the most was her complete conviction that he was such a stuffed shirt.

At one time Jonathan would have been pleased by that character assessment. A conservative, serious businessman was exactly the kind of image he wanted to project. Jonathan's good looks had been more of a hindrance than a help in his chosen field of corporate tax law, so he'd deliberately toned down his appearance with glasses and an ultraconservative wardrobe. The technique had been very successful. His ascent up the corporate ladder was currently progressing at a rewarding pace. But now Jonathan couldn't help wondering if the image had overpowered the man. Had he actually become as sober, steady, and sedate as he pretended to be?

Disconcerted by his train of thought, Jonathan's dark blue eyes scanned over the scattered crowd sitting on the other side of the glass partition that formed the back wall of the racquetball court. He'd left his dark-framed glasses in his locker and was now wearing soft contact lenses. The change in his appearance was immense.

Dan Moore, his racquetball partner, was nowhere in sight. However, Jonathan's visual search did put him in eye contact with a gorgeous blonde who was seated on the wide, carpeted steps that formed a bleacher-type waiting and observation area. The woman's athletic shorts were minimal and her T-shirt provocatively tight. Jonathan flashed her an approving grin and received an equally approving wink plus a smile in return.

Good, he thought to himself. *I haven't lost my touch. Maybe after the match . . .* Jonathan's speculative thoughts were interrupted by his friend's arrival.

"Hey, sorry I'm late," Dan apologized as he hurriedly dropped his racquet bag in the back corner of the court.

"No problem." Jonathan was still eyeing the blonde.

"I see you've gathered an audience," Dan noted.

"Yeah, must be my flashy forehand."

"Must be. You ready for this match?"

"Ready."

"Loser buys drinks, right?" Dan offered.

"You got it. I hope you brought your wallet," Jonathan said as he prepared to serve the first throw. The black athletic shorts and loose-fitting sweat top he wore not only accentuated his good looks, they also allowed him freedom of movement. His powerful body was extended to his full height of six feet three inches as he arched his arm back to hit the ball with controlled force. The muscles of his upper thighs tightened as he immediately crouched into position, waiting for Dan to return the ball.

Jonathan's concentration was intense as he channeled all of his earlier frustration into his playing.

Even though the match didn't take long—Jonathan won

all three games—the promising-looking blonde had disappeared by the time Jonathan and Dan left the court.

"Something happen this weekend or what?" Dan demanded in a weary voice as he and Jonathan made their way to the men's showers. "That was no friendly game of racquetball we just played. You were out for blood!"

"I was playing for a round of free drinks, remember?" Jonathan countered.

"I remember." The shower helped to revive Dan's spirits. Over the noise of rushing water he shouted, "Listen, I hope you don't mind if we have the drinks with some friends of mine?"

"No problem," Jonathan shouted back from the next shower stall.

It was nearing five o'clock by the time Jonathan and Dan regrouped in front of The Lion's Inn Pub. They paused just inside the door while their eyes adjusted to the pub's cozy darkness. The place was crowded. Every stool around the bar was taken. The overflow stood behind, all cheering the last inning of a baseball game being shown on a large-screen television.

"Busy place," Jonathan noted.

"Yeah, it's happy hour," Dan explained. "Drinks are two for one from now until six."

They'd almost walked past the bar area when Dan suddenly stopped and said, "Wait a second. There's someone I'd like you to meet." Dan put his hands to his mouth and yelled, "Yo, Erin!"

Erin turned at the sound of her name. She located Dan across the crowded room and waved a hand to show she'd heard him.

Dan's broad back blocked Jonathan's view until they were only a few feet away from Erin. Even then, the end section of the L-shaped bar still concealed most of her figure. But Jonathan would have recognized that face anywhere.

"Hey, Erin, here's somebody I want you to meet. Jonathan Garrett, this is Erin Rossi."

Dan watched in surprise as both Jonathan and Erin stiffened with displeasure before simultaneously drawling, "We've already met!"

Smiling distantly at Erin, Jonathan said, "Would you excuse us for a moment, please?" Jonathan hustled Dan aside, stopping once they were safely out of Erin's hearing. "You're not trying to fix me up with your friend Erin, are you?" Jonathan demanded. He'd been the target of matchmaking attempts before.

Dan actually smiled at Jonathan's accusation. "No way. Erin already has a hard time keeping track of the men in her life."

"Really?" Jonathan obviously found that hard to believe.

"Really. One look at her and you'll know why."

Jonathan frowned at Dan and took another look at Erin. She'd just stepped away from the bar with a trayful of drinks in her hands. A moment later Jonathan got his first eyeful of the real Erin Rossi. Her figure was even better than the blonde's at the health club! She was wearing a pair of khaki-colored Bermuda shorts that molded her bottom and left the long, tanned expanse of her legs bare all the way down to the leather moccasins she wore. As she turned to maneuver her way around a table, Jonathan saw her side view, which displayed the thrust of her breasts beneath her brilliant red shirt.

Unaware of Jonathan's surprise, Dan continued speaking. "Besides, you and Erin really don't have anything in common."

Keeping his eyes glued to Erin, Jonathan murmured, "Haven't you heard that opposites attract?"

"The only thing opposites attract is trouble," Dan maintained.

"Maybe," Jonathan softly agreed. "But from where I'm standing, this trouble looks mighty appealing."

"Does that mean our private discussion is over?" Dan asked with wry humor.

"Yes." Jonathan's nod was decisive. "Lead on."

Dan took Jonathan over to meet his group of friends, who were all seated in the back corner of the pub. Erin was still standing, passing out drinks from the tray she'd brought from the bar. Watching her, Jonathan suddenly realized that Erin might be employed by the pub as well as by the dry cleaners.

Dan raised his voice in order to be heard over the surrounding din. "Everybody, I'd like you to meet a friend of mine. This is Jonathan Garrett, a tax attorney who plays a deadly game of racquetball. Jonathan, this is Paul, Martha, Ned, Wanda . . ." Dan kept pointing all the way around the table until he'd named everyone present.

After the introductions were made and Jonathan was engaged in conversation with Martha, it was Erin's turn to tug Dan aside for a private conversation. "This is the guy you told me would be perfect for the male lead?" Erin demanded in disbelief.

Dan nodded. "He's the one. But I haven't told him yet that he's meeting the central core of the Village Players."

Before she could respond, Erin's attention was being demanded by someone at the table.

"Erin!" Martha grabbed her by the hand and brought her back to sit right next to Jonathan. Martha may have looked like a sweet old grandmother, but actually she was a sharp realtor who preferred action over words. "Our troubles are over!"

"Really?" Erin asked, surprised by the hum of excitement

in the air. Everyone around the table was looking at her with obvious expectancy. Everyone, that is, except Jonathan, who was looking at her with an expression she was too busy to interpret.

Paul eagerly leaned across the table to speak to Erin. "Jonathan would be perfect. He's got the look. Don't you think so?"

"Perfect for what?" Jonathan demanded suspiciously, suddenly feeling some misgivings at the other man's speculative appraisal.

"How familiar are you with *The Importance of Being Earnest?*" someone else asked Jonathan.

Jonathan was stymied. "Earnest as in *truthful?*"

"No. Earnest as in the play by Oscar Wilde," Erin explained. "*The Importance of Being Earnest.*"

"I think I may have read it in high school," Jonathan replied. "Why?"

"*Importance* is our next production," Erin told him.

"Production?" Jonathan looked surprised. "You mean, you're actors?"

"That's right. We're members of the Village Players. No need to look so shocked, Mr. Garrett." Erin's voice was mocking.

"My name is Jonathan, and I'm not shocked, Erin." He sent her a meaningful look as he softly added, "I don't shock easily."

"No?" she retorted. "You could have fooled me."

He had fooled her, Jonathan realized. Fooled her into believing the role he was playing. He absently fingered the frames of his glasses, wondering if he should slip them off. But something about Erin's attitude spurred him into continuing the charade. She was so sure she had him pegged.

"Have you ever done any acting?" Martha asked Jonathan.

"Not really, no." He could hardly admit that he was acting every day in his role of corporate tax attorney.

"You should try it," Martha suggested. "I'm sure you'd be good."

Erin studied Jonathan while he conversed with Martha. Strange, she hadn't really bothered to look at him when he'd come into the dry cleaners. All she'd noticed were his glasses, his height, and his authoritative voice. Now she paused to take stock of the rest of him.

Erin started with Jonathan's profile. His dark-framed glasses were the dominating factor, but once she looked beyond them, she noted that his nose was aquiline, the planes of his face surprisingly angular. Unfortunately she still couldn't determine the color of his eyes.

Although no longer wearing a three-piece suit, Jonathan was still more formally dressed than the other men around the table. He wore a pale blue shirt, and he had broader shoulders than she'd remembered. A discriminating maroon silk tie was neatly tied beneath his shirt collar. All Erin could tell about his trousers was that they were dark and fit him well.

Moving on, Erin focused her attention on Jonathan's hands as he accepted a bottle of imported beer from Dan. He had artist's hands. His fingers were long and symmetrical. What was a lawyer doing with hands like that? she wondered, somewhat disgruntled by the discovery.

Martha's voice cut into Erin's thoughts. "Don't you agree, Erin?"

Erin blinked and refocused her attention on Martha. "What?"

"I was saying that Jonathan should come to the auditions tomorrow night and read for the part of John Worthing," Martha repeated. "Don't you agree?"

Erin immediately dismissed the idea. Mr. Stuffed Shirt, himself, regardless of how artistic his hands looked, would never demean himself by acting. "I'm sure Mr. Garrett wouldn't be interested in doing that."

"On the contrary," Jonathan said, taking great pleasure in contradicting her. "I would be very interested."

"The auditions are tomorrow night," Erin pointed out. "That hardly gives you time to prepare."

Every member of the Village Players present sent Erin a look of bewilderment at her reluctance to invite Jonathan to the open audition. It was a well known fact that their acting group was short of men—most community theater groups were. The standing joke among them all was that any man who could breathe and read was accepted and in like Flynn. So why was Erin discouraging Jonathan from auditioning?

It was a question Erin was asking herself as well. The answer, she told herself, was simple. There would be enough problems arising during the course of the eight-week rehearsal period without asking for trouble by teaming her with Jonathan Garrett.

Dan was the first to speak to Erin, and he said only two words. "Remember Wally."

A retired math teacher, Wally was a fellow member of the theater group, the husband of the Village Players' reigning president, Freda Humphries. Freda was forever trying to cast her husband in leading roles. Unfortunately Wally had two major drawbacks—he couldn't act worth a damn, and he couldn't remember his lines. But that didn't stop him from auditioning for every lead. And if no one else auditioned for the role of John Worthing, it was possible that the group's worst nightmare could come true. Wally might actually be the only candidate for one of the lead roles.

The warning was all Erin needed. "If you want to audition, Mr. Garrett, then of course you're welcome to come to the Little Theatre tomorrow night."

"Thank you for the invitation." Jonathan's voice was solemn.

Erin eyed him suspiciously. "Don't mention it."

"Where is this little theater and what time should I be there?" Jonathan asked.

Dan gave him directions. "You can't miss it. We've got a sign out front that says Village Players' Little Theatre."

"You'll see why we call it the Little Theatre as soon as you get there," Martha inserted.

"The building used to be a one-room schoolhouse," Dan explained. "Our space is limited, but we hope to expand within the next five years. Anyway, auditions begin at seven. I just happen to have an extra copy of the play you can look over tonight so you can get a feel for the character of John Worthing." Dan pulled the play from the athletic bag he'd brought into the pub with him and handed the script to Jonathan.

"Be sure to take note of the subtitle," Erin suggested.

Jonathan read the words with an inward smile. *A trivial comedy for serious people.* Another sign of her opinion of him. Her certainty about him was a challenge he couldn't refuse. "What do I do at this audition?"

"Nothing radical," Erin mockingly assured him. "All you'll have to do is read whatever lines the director and producer have chosen."

"By the way, I'm the producer," Dan said.

"Really? Who's the director?" Jonathan asked.

"I am." The words came from Erin.

Jonathan's brows rose in surprise. "You are?"

"Still interested?" she taunted.

23

"Fascinated," he returned. "I wouldn't have thought you'd have the time to direct a play, what with your job here and at the dry cleaners."

Now it was Erin's turn to look surprised. "My job here?"

"You're not a waitress?"

"That's correct. I am not a waitress."

"Then you only work at the dry cleaners?"

"No."

"No, what?"

"I don't work at the dry cleaners, either."

"But I saw you there yesterday."

"That's true."

Jonathan was getting impatient now. "Well, if you don't work there, what were you doing wearing a baggy smock that said 'Courtesy Cleaners'?"

"I was filling in for my parents. They own the cleaners."

"Erin's a graphic artist," Martha volunteered, thereby saving Jonathan the effort of having to pry more information from Erin.

"She's also a brand-new aunt," someone else offered. "How's your niece doing, by the way?"

"Great!" Thinking about the baby made Erin smile. "She's got the cutest little prune face."

"Don't let your sister hear you talking like that," Martha warned. "A new mother does not appreciate hearing her pride and joy referred to as prune-faced."

"My sister Mary was the first one to call her prune-faced," Erin retorted.

"Outspokenness must run in your family," Jonathan noted with a meaningful look.

Dan observed the unspoken communication between his two friends with some degree of curiosity. Under cover of the group discussion about babies Dan directed a quiet question to Erin. "You never did tell me where you and Jonathan met."

Afterward Erin told herself that she would never have answered so outspokenly had it not been for the smug look she caught on Jonathan's face. That look was enough to make her want to rattle his cage. "Jonathan lost his pants, and I had to help him find them."

Contrary to her expectations, Jonathan showed no signs of discomfort. "That's right," he agreed, as if Erin's description of their meeting were commonplace.

The only one looking confused was Dan. "I see. And where did this take place, if it wouldn't be too presumptuous of me to ask?"

"You're a producer now, Dan," Erin mockingly assured him. "You can be as presumptuous as you like."

"Yeah, right." Dan's inflection was wry.

"Erin and I met at her parents' dry cleaners yesterday," Jonathan replied on her behalf.

Something about the way Jonathan relayed the information made Dan wonder if Erin weren't the reason behind Jonathan's driven game of racquetball. Even a blind man could see the sparks flying between Jonathan and Erin at the moment.

Aware of Dan's suddenly speculative stare, Erin called upon her own acting abilities to mask her feelings. Entering into the group's discussion, she smiled and joked, argued and laughed, as she always did whenever the Village Players got together. By the time the group was ready to call it a night, Dan couldn't help wondering if he'd imagined the earlier friction between Erin and Jonathan.

Jonathan knew better. He was well aware of Erin's act. He'd viewed it silently, biding his time, fully intending to speak to Erin privately once the group had left. But he hadn't anticipated Erin's smooth retreat.

"See you all tomorrow night." She addressed her farewell to the group and slipped off so quickly that she was gone before Jonathan could stop her.

Pleased with her exit, Erin slid into the driver's seat of her mini-van and popped a classical cassette into her stereo tape deck before starting the van. The Vivaldi tape was almost over by the time she pulled into the gravel drive next to her home. The gatehouse had been hers for two months now, and she still had a hard time believing her luck in finding it.

She deliberately kept her thoughts off Jonathan Garrett as she entered her home through the rounded turretlike enclosure that housed the front door. The matching turret on the other front corner of the cottage held the dining room's bow window. The eccentric castlelike architecture suited Erin perfectly. After living in boxlike apartments she found the numerous nooks and crannies in her new home to be a positive delight.

The cottage had once been the gatehouse for a large estate. The present-day owners had recently decided to rent it out, and Erin had been lucky enough to be in the right place at the right time.

There was only one unusual stipulation to her lease, and that was that she had to share the place with Butch—a twenty-two-pound tomcat!

At first Erin had had some trouble adjusting to Butch's quirks. His fascination with television, especially football games, was one thing. But his Machiavellian interest in the contents of her lingerie drawers was something else again. She'd finally had to resort to locking her silky nightwear away in a refurbished steamer trunk that she used as a bedside table.

The steamer trunk, like every piece of furniture Erin had

selected to furnish her home, had a story behind it. The trunk had originally been used by a touring company of actors before it had been abandoned in an antique warehouse, waiting for Erin to come along and rescue it. She was still saving up for her next acquisition, an antique solid brass bed. She had only two more payments to make on the layaway plan and it would be hers.

Erin kicked off her moccasins as soon as she was inside. No matter how comfortable her shoes might be, she still preferred being barefoot. Reaching out with one hand, she flicked on the old-fashioned brass lamp in the living room.

Butch blinked sleepily against the sudden glare of light. His orange-and-white fur stood out against the deep maroon upholstery of the overstuffed chair he was curled up on. Yawning, Butch got up and stretched languidly. He then jumped down onto the handwoven cream-colored cotton rug that covered most of the natural wood floor in the living room.

Erin was able to keep her thoughts away from Jonathan as she opened a can of cat food for Butch's evening meal. But when she got into bed later that night, she couldn't help wondering about tomorrow night's auditions.

"This is ridiculous!" she declared after reading the same page of her copy of *The Importance of Being Earnest* for the fourth time and still not absorbing any of the words. After turning off her bedside lamp Erin spoke into the darkness. "I'm not going to lose any sleep over that man!"

In his town house several miles away, Jonathan was also reading *The Importance of Being Earnest*, because he was determined to get the role tomorrow—and Erin soon thereafter!

CHAPTER THREE

"Her . . . mother is . . . perfectly . . . unbearable. Never met such . . . a . . . a . . . a . . . gargoyle!"

Erin interrupted Wally's halting recitation. "Excuse me, Wally, but the line should read *gorgon*, not gargoyle."

Wally shrugged indifferently. "Gargoyle—gorgon, what's the difference? I was just going good, Erin. You shouldn't have interrupted me. Now I'll have to start all over again."

"That's really not necessary, Wally," Erin hurriedly assured him. "I think you've already given us a fairly good idea of your interpretation of the role."

Wally had read two other scenes in the play involving interaction with different characters. Erin, Wanda, the stage manager, and Dan had all quietly sat through Wally's awkward performance.

"We'll let you know when we've made our decision," Erin promised.

Wally nodded confidently and moved away to consult with his wife, Freda.

The turnout for the open rehearsal was good. Over fifteen people had shown up to read for the nine parts available in the Oscar Wilde play. Five of the parts were for males; four for females. As director, the casting fell under Erin's domain, but she welcomed input from both Wanda and Dan. The three exchanged their opinions of each person's audition by writing brief notes and sliding them along the table they sat behind.

So far Erin had decided on seven of the roles. The only remaining openings were for the leading role of John Worthing and the love of his life, Gwendolen Fairfax. Both roles had only two people reading for them. Two women, both veteran actresses with the Village Players, had already auditioned for the role of Gwen, and both were so good that Erin needed more time to choose between them. As for the character of John Worthing, Wally had already botched his reading. Now it was Jonathan's turn.

"Mr. Garrett, we're ready for you." *Or as ready as I'll ever be*, Erin silently tacked on as she watched Jonathan come forward. She knew he'd been observing the auditions from one of the metal chairs set along the wall. She'd been disturbingly aware of his presence from the moment he'd stepped into the Little Theatre at precisely five minutes to seven.

Two things set Jonathan apart from the others. First, his dark three-piece suit stood out in the mostly blue-jeaned crowd. He didn't even unbutton his jacket or loosen his tie. Secondly, Jonathan appeared to be cool, calm, and in control. He didn't display any of the nervousness that people usually experienced at their first audition, or any audition for that matter. Jonathan simply possessed that unruffled look of a well-to-do English gentleman so necessary for the character of John Worthing.

Erin watched Jonathan's movements closely as he walked toward her. For such a tall man he moved with smooth coordination. The Little Theatre's thrust stage was not overly large, and Erin had thought that Jonathan's height might make him appear out of proportion with his surroundings. But that wasn't the case.

Erin jotted her observations on the side of Jonathan's audition form. While doing so she took a moment to study Jonathan's handwriting. Although clearly readable, it wasn't as pristinely neat as she might have expected. The strokes were bold and authoritative, yet he crossed his *t*'s with an unexpected flair. The form asked for name, address, evening phone number, previous acting or theater experience, and the name of the play and character under consideration. Erin could tell from Jonathan's address that he must be doing well as a tax attorney.

While Erin was making these silent observations Dan was speaking to Jonathan. "What do you think of our Little Theatre?"

"It's not quite what I expected," Jonathan admitted.

"Don't let the lack of a raised stage throw you," Dan said. "Consider this to be a sort of theater in the round, except that the audience sits on three sides instead of all four."

Since Jonathan had not had much time to prepare, Erin thought it only fair to explain the first scene she'd chosen for him to read. "We'll begin with the scene on page twenty," she told him. "Were you able to read the play last night?"

"Yes."

"Good. Then I'll only describe the action briefly. You've just asked Gwendolen to marry you and are now being cross-examined by Gwendolen's mother, Lady Bracknell, as to your suitability as a husband. Martha will be reading the lines for Lady Bracknell."

Martha was also Erin's choice for the role of Lady Bracknell in the play, and Erin wanted to see how she and Jonathan interacted on stage.

"Do you have any questions?" Erin asked Jonathan.

He shook his head.

"You may begin whenever you're ready. Martha, please start with 'You may take a seat, Mr. Worthing.' "

Martha read her line and the audition began. Erin critiqued Jonathan's performance on several levels. She listened to the quality of his voice as he read his lines with certainty and ease. He projected well, and his enunciation was excellent. She watched his body language, noted his facial expressions. And she knew within the first few moments that this was their John Worthing.

Erin asked Jonathan to read two more scenes. One involved Paul, who would be playing John Worthing's friend, Algernon Moncrieff. The other scene included the women who would be playing the role of John Worthing's young ward, Cecily, and Miss Prism, her teacher. In all instances Jonathan blended well with the other actors, giving Erin a preview of how the ensemble would look together on stage.

Although Erin had already made most of her casting decisions, tradition decreed that she wait and notify everyone personally. The procedure cut down on hurt egos.

"Thank you, Jonathan. We'll be in touch with you." She then shifted her attention to the group of people who'd already auditioned. "Thank you all for showing up at our open audition. I'd appreciate it if everyone would take note of the rehearsal schedule I passed out earlier. Doing a play takes a lot of work and commitment. Cast members will be required to spend several evenings a week and Saturdays at the theater during the eight-week rehearsal period. So keep that in mind. End of lecture! We'll be contacting everyone tomorrow evening with the casting decisions."

As the group prepared to depart Erin added a few more notes to those she'd already written about the numerous people she'd seen perform. She still wasn't sure which woman to cast as Gwendolen. She liked each of the actresses for different reasons. Before they left she made arrangements for them both to come back tomorrow evening so that she could see them again.

Feeling the need for a bracing cup of coffee, Erin headed over to the card table that had been set up with a portable coffee maker and Styrofoam cups. Luckily she liked her coffee black, but even so, she grimaced at the strong brew.

"You remind me of a rabbit when you do that," Jonathan noted as he joined her. "You made a face like that when Wally was doing his reading."

"I did?"

Jonathan nodded.

The seconds slowly dragged by without another word being spoken. Uncomfortable with the silence, Erin launched into conversation. "So, was your first audition as bad as you anticipated?"

"Not at all," he replied.

"Good."

"Was I?"

"What?"

"Good."

"You've got potential. Do you wear your glasses all the time?" she abruptly asked him.

"I wear contacts when I play racquetball, but they irritate my eyes if I wear them all the time."

Erin frowned at the news. "Would that be a problem if you got the role? You'd have to wear the contacts during the performance and for the rehearsals leading up to that time. John Worthing doesn't wear glasses."

"Couldn't I keep my glasses on for the first few weeks of rehearsals?"

"You sound like your glasses are your security blanket."

"I don't feel comfortable without them," Jonathan stated in an implacable voice.

"You're going to have to be without them for the performance," Erin pointed out impatiently. "Does that mean you're going to be uncomfortable throughout the play? Because if so, I need to know that ahead of time, Mr. Garrett. It will affect my casting decision. Come to think of it, maybe I should have asked you to remove your glasses during your audition. I have no idea how you'll look without them. You'd better take them off now so I can check it out."

Erin viewed his disconcerted expression with some amusement. "Come on, Jonathan. I'm asking you to take off your glasses, not your trousers. There's no need to be embarrassed. Here, I'll do it for you." She reached up and slid the dark frames away from his face.

His eyes were blue. Dark blue. She noted that much before he squinted in an apparent effort to see her.

"You really shouldn't be afraid to take off your glasses," she chastised him. "You're not such a bad looking guy that you have to hide behind them."

Her comment was meant to soothe his ruffled feathers, but it had the opposite effect. Jonathan grabbed his glasses from her and jammed them back onto his nose. "Thank you so much for the psychology lesson." His voice was coated with sarcasm.

"*Jeeez. Excuuuuse meee,*" Erin muttered as he stormed out of the theater.

"Your friend Jonathan sure is sensitive," Erin informed Dan as she rejoined him and Wanda at their worktable.

"Why? What did you say to him?"

Erin shrugged her shoulders. "I gave him a compliment, and he acted like I'd insulted him or something."

Dan repeated his question, more specifically this time. "What *exactly* did you say to him?"

"That he wasn't so bad-looking that he had to hide behind his glasses. . . . What are you laughing at?" she demanded as Dan cracked up.

Dan wiped the mirth tears from his eyes. "I'll have you know that most women find Jonathan very attractive."

"Really? I guess it takes all kinds." She dismissed the subject with another shrug. "Listen, can we get back to work here? Let's review what I've decided so far." Erin consulted her notes. "Paul is Algernon, Roger is Merriman the butler, Ken is Lane the butler, and Artie is Reverend Chausible. Martha is Lady Bracknell, Cindy is Cecily Cardew, and Betty is Miss Prism. I'd like callbacks on Jonathan as John Worthing and both Sue and Deidre as Gwendolen."

Erin made most of the calls herself the next day right after work. She knew from her own experience that waiting to hear after an audition was nerve-racking, so she tried to get back to people as soon as possible. Erin left Jonathan's call for the last.

His hello sounded unconcerned.

"Jonathan, this is Erin Rossi. We'd like you to come back to the Little Theatre and do another reading for us."

Jonathan was still smarting from Erin's offhand assurance that he wasn't so bad-looking that he needed to hide behind his glasses. But once he'd recovered from his initial anger, he was more determined than ever to continue with his deception. "When?"

"Would you be able to come this evening at around eight-thirty?"

"Yes."

"Fine, we'll see you then."

Erin hung up the phone, feeling slightly disgruntled and unable to put her finger on why she felt that way. Jonathan hadn't said anything wrong. In fact, he'd hardly said anything at all, and maybe that was what bothered her.

At the theater later that night, Erin had Jonathan read lines with both Sue and Deidre. It was a hard choice, but Erin decided to follow her instincts and go with Sue.

As for Jonathan, there was still one more acting hurdle she needed him to overcome. "I'd like you to do a bit of pantomime," Erin requested.

"Pantomime?"

"Yes. I'd like you to pretend you're picking up a large dog. Then I'd like you to carry the dog over to the other side of the stage and give him a bath."

Jonathan looked at Erin as if she were crazy.

"It's not as strange a request as it sounds," Dan hastened to intercede. "Look on it as a sort of mini acting display."

"I need to judge your physical flexibility and imagination," Erin explained.

"I'm sure there are other, more satisfactory ways of testing those attributes," Jonathan said with such a straight face that Erin couldn't be sure if his comment held sexual overtones or not.

"I'm sure there are," she retorted, "but this is the one we're going to use."

"I'll look ridiculous," he protested.

"No more ridiculous than you looked throwing a fit in my parents' dry cleaners," Erin assured him.

Jonathan did the requested pantomime, but he clearly wasn't happy about it.

Erin could see he had potential and told him so. "You just need to lighten up a bit. Don't take life so seriously! Try and learn a little *joie de vivre!*"

Her comment was exactly the cue Jonathan was waiting for. "Teach me."

"What?"

"Teach me how to have fun."

"You can't be serious."

"I'm perfectly serious," he assured her.

"Having fun isn't something anyone can teach you. It's a state of mind."

"So's meditation," Jonathan retorted, "but a good teacher

can train someone how to meditate."

His entire attitude was a challenge Erin couldn't refuse. "Fine. If you want to have fun, I'll show you how. Only let me make something clear. This is nothing personal. I'm simply willing to open your mind in the best interests of the play."

"Understood." Jonathan kept his satisfaction to himself. "When's our first lesson?"

"Are you busy tomorrow night?"

He mentally reviewed his calendar. "No, I'm not busy."

"Fine. Lesson one begins tomorrow night. I don't suppose you happen to own a bowling ball, do you?"

"No. Why? What kind of fun are you planning on having with a bowling ball?"

Erin had to laugh at Jonathan's wary expression. "Nothing kinky. I thought we'd bowl a few games at a bowling alley."

Jonathan did not look thrilled at the prospect.

"What's wrong?" she taunted. "You did say you wanted to have fun, didn't you?"

"Yes. But bowling is not my idea of fun."

"I know. No doubt your idea of fun is reading an Internal Revenue Handbook, which is why you need a teacher in the *joie-de-vivre* department."

"Actually it's called 'The Internal Revenue Code and Regulations' but it's not the only thing I read," Jonathan stated, playing his role to the hilt. "I also read the stock reports in *The Wall Street Journal.*"

Erin merely groaned. "Just meet me at the Star Bowling Alley tomorrow night at eight." She gave him directions before adding, "We can rent bowling balls and shoes there."

Erin hadn't been to the Star Bowling Alley for a while and was surprised the next evening to find a neon sign proudly stating that it was under new management. As a teenager she'd participated in junior bowling leagues at the Star and had even won the championship one year. But as she got older and other things became more important in her life, she had less time for bowling.

The parking lot was unexpectedly crowded. The new management must be doing something right to boost business so much, Erin decided as she swung around a row of parked cars, looking for an empty space. She finally found one and pulled into it, glad that her Voyager mini-van was the size of a standard station wagon and didn't need a lot of space. A second later a dark sedan pulled in across from her and Jonathan got out.

"You're in a suit!" Erin moaned in dismay.

The parking lot lights reflected off Jonathan's glasses as he nodded. "I got tied up at work and didn't have time to change. It's no big deal, is it?"

"No, of course not," Erin muttered half under her breath. "Everyone goes bowling in a three-piece suit!"

"I'll take off the jacket once we get inside," Jonathan promised.

"Great. I can hardly wait," Erin was so concerned with Jonathan's formal attire that she didn't pay attention to the overabundance of motorcycles and battered pickup trucks in the parking lot. Her first inkling of trouble came when she stepped through the darkened glass door Jonathan held open for her. The smoke inside the bowling alley cut down the visibility drastically, and the smell was overwhelming. Stale beer and dirty socks. Blinking rapidly, Erin attempted to squint through the haze. What she saw made her wish her vision had remained clouded.

The bowling alley bore no resemblance to the way it had been the last time she'd visited it a year ago. A couple of pool tables had been added to one side, the bar had doubled in size, and an adult video rental desk stood next to the door.

"Nice ambience," Jonathan noted as he studied his surroundings, much as an anthropologist would a foreign culture.

A man with a glassful of beer bumped into them without apology as he made his weaving way over to his pals. Jonathan read the message across the back of the man's shirt. "Rosslyn Funeral Homes"?

"It must be league night," Erin explained.

"Oh? I thought this was a result of the full moon."

Jonathan gave a pointed look at another passerby who sported a ragged beard and a series of tattoos that ran from his bared upper arm right down to his west.

"Very funny. Look, it was a mistake bringing you here." It was a mistake bringing anyone here, she decided as a fight broke out in the pool hall. "Let's get out of here."

"So soon?" Jonathan questioned with mocking regret. "And it was just getting interesting."

"The place is under new management," Erin angrily stated as she stalked to her red Voyager. "It wasn't like that the last time I was here."

"Does that mean that what we viewed was not your idea of fun?"

"No."

"Just checking." Jonathan waited until she'd unlocked her door before opening it for her. "Now what?"

He was standing so close to her that she could feel his presence. "I suppose we could go to another bowling alley," Erin heard herself saying.

"There's one in my neighborhood," Jonathan said. "I happened to notice it as I drove to work this morning."

And knowing that Jonathan lived in a pretty ritzy neighborhood, Erin expected that the place should be of a higher caliber than the Star Bowling Alley apparently had become.

"All right. Drive on, I'll follow you."

Thankfully the second bowling alley was nothing like the first. This one wasn't even called an alley but instead was advertised as a bowling center. A sign near the door proclaimed that on Wednesday night open bowling was allowed after nine P.M. It was a little after that now.

The place wasn't overly crowded or smoky. They didn't have to wait but were assigned a lane right away.

"We'll need to rent shoes," Erin told the attendant.

"What size?"

"Size sevens for me." Erin turned to Jonathan inquiringly.

"Tens."

The attendant handed over two pairs of shoes whose soles were soft, to protect the wood floors near the bowling lanes and to cut down on skidding. "That'll be two dollars."

"We'll go Dutch," Erin insisted as she reached into her oversize purse in search of her wallet.

"No, we won't." Jonathan pulled out his wallet and handed over the money with efficient speed.

"You're in lane forty-seven," the attendant told them.

Erin led Jonathan over to their assigned lane and dumped her purse and bowling bag on one of the plastic seats. She then peeled off the thin jacket she'd worn. Although August was one of Portland's warmest months, the nights still got cool. Her jeans were of the stretch variety, to allow for the most freedom of movement. And her shirt was black with large hot-pink polka dots.

Jonathan shielded his eyes with his hands. "I think I'm going to need sunglasses."

"This is my lucky bowling shirt," Erin explained without the least bit of self-consciousness. "Whenever I wear it I win."

"I can understand why." Jonathan nodded sagaciously.

"You blind the other bowlers so they can't see what they're doing."

"Listen, people in glass houses shouldn't throw stones. You're the one who's not dressed for the occasion. In case you hadn't noticed, no one else here is even wearing a tie, let alone an entire suit."

"I'll take off my jacket and tie," Jonathan offered. He removed his dark blue serge suit jacket and carefully hung it over the back of one of the seats. Aware of Erin's scrutiny, Jonathan removed his tie with equal care and draped that over the jacket.

"Come on, Jonathan. Loosen up! Take off the vest too. I promise not to swoon."

"You're sure?"

"I'm positive."

He removed his vest.

Erin simply shook her head at his white shirt. "I guess that's the best we can do. Just out of curiosity, you don't play racquetball in a suit, do you?"

"No."

"Good. Then I suppose there's some hope for you after all. Come on, I'll show you where the bowling balls are. I've brought my own, but you'll have to choose one from the racks here."

"All bowling balls look the same to me," Jonathan said as he stared at them.

"Okay, I'll help you. Stick out your hand."

"What for?"

"Talk about suspicious . . ." Erin shook her head at him and clucked her disapproval as she took hold of Jonathan's right hand herself.

Erin had never been self-conscious with men, either physically or verbally. Yet, as she felt the warmth and strength of

Jonathan's fingers for the first time, she was thrown by her unexpected response. Her fingertips felt singed. Erin frowned at them. What was wrong with her? Even worse was the irrational pleasure kicking her heartbeat into high gear.

"Something wrong?" Jonathan asked, viewing her confused face with bland innocence. He was getting to her! He knew it. And his instincts in these matters were always correct.

"Uh, nothing." Erin shook her head as if to clear it of disruptive images. "Where was I?"

"You were holding my hand. You still are."

"I'm merely checking your span," Erin loftily informed him.

"Really?" Jonathan had a hard time keeping a straight face. "And how is my *span* doing?"

"You've got long fingers, which means you need a bowling ball with a wide span, a lot of space between the finger and thumb holes." Erin was proud of the way she casually reeled off that information before nonchalantly dropping Jonathan's hand. She then turned away from him to study the rack of bowling balls, thereby missing the gleam of satisfaction in Jonathan's eyes.

"Here, try this one," she suggested, handing him a black bowling ball. "Is that too heavy? It's a sixteen-pounder. I couldn't find one that weighs less."

Does she think I'm a weakling? Jonathan thought to himself with humorous irritation. "My briefcase usually weighs more than this," he retorted. "I don't think I'll have any trouble."

When they returned to their lane, Erin unzipped her bowling bag and pulled out her custom-designed bowling ball. Her father had given it to her for her fifteenth birthday.

41

She carefully placed her ball on the automatic ball-return rack and indicated that Jonathan should do the same with his.

"Now, the first thing a bowler does when it's time to roll is to pick up the ball, and there's only one really safe way of doing that." As Erin bent over to demonstrate she looked over her shoulder to make sure Jonathan was paying attention. Convinced that he was, she resumed her gaze forward. "You put one hand firmly on each side of the ball, get a good grip on it, then lift the ball and cradle it in one arm and against your body."

The moment Erin stopped monitoring Jonathan, he shifted his attention from the metal ball-return to the much more tempting lines of Erin's body. Her jeans molded her trim bottom as she bent over. When she cradled the bowling ball against her body, Jonathan longed to trade places with the piece of sporting equipment.

"Did you get that?" she demanded, turning to face him.

"I got it." His voice was slightly raspy.

"Then you pick up your ball."

Jonathan did so with no trouble.

"Now put your fingers in like this." Erin inserted her fingers and her thumb into the corresponding triangularly placed holes in her bowling ball. "Index and middle fingers first, thumb last. Fine. For most people the conventional three-holed grip is the best." *You're babbling,* Erin silently reprimanded herself. *Stop staring at his fingers. So the man's got great hands. Big deal! Concentrate on your bowling. Remember to plan your approach and release.* Erin almost groaned at the sexual connotations the bowling terms suddenly evoked. Her palms became sweaty and her breathing shallow. "Watch me, and then do exactly as I do," she instructed.

"Okay."

Despite Erin's best intentions, Jonathan's unwavering attention threw her concentration. The ball swerved off course and ended up in the gutter.

Jonathan looked down the sixty-foot lane and then back to Erin. "I'm no expert at this game, but isn't the object to knock over some of those white pins at the end there?"

"Very funny." She glared at him. "You try it."

Jonathan did, with slightly better results. He actually knocked down five of the ten pins.

Erin noted Jonathan's score on the score sheet. "Keeping score is part of the fun of the game," she said before going on to explain the intricacies of scoring spares and strikes.

"You lost me. Tax laws sound less complicated than this," Jonathan stated. "You be scorekeeper. I trust you."

As the game progressed, their scores improved. Erin found that Jonathan was a fast learner. He moved well. She liked that.

Erin was watching him as he prepared to bowl his next game. Facing the pins at the end of the lane, he stood with his back to her. The flesh tone of his skin was a shadowy suggestion beneath the smooth broadcloth of his shirt. Without his suit jacket and vest she was able to appreciate how truly broad and powerful his back was. Erin studied Jonathan intently, determined to discover why she'd reacted so strongly when she'd held his hand. Now that she looked closely, she realized his body wasn't bad for a stuffed shirt!

Although not coy, Erin had no desire to get caught staring blatantly at Jonathan, so she shifted her eyes to the bowling pins just in time to see them all fall. "A strike! You got a strike!" In an instant Erin's natural enthusiasm had her out of her seat and racing toward Jonathan. Without a second thought she engulfed him in a bear hug.

"Congratulations!" Her voice was breathless from her

mad dash, or at least that was the excuse she gave herself.

Jonathan gazed down in delight at Erin's animated face. He had her where he wanted her—in his arms. His first instinct was to kiss her, to pull her even closer and explore the warmth of her mouth. But he couldn't do that without blowing his stuffed shirt cover. So he had to fight temptation and reluctantly loosen his hold on her.

As Erin stepped away from him she fervently wished the lenses of his glasses weren't such an effective camouflage. She also wished she felt as calm and collected as he looked. Why was she so shaken up inside? Shrugging off her perplexity, Erin returned to her role of scorekeeper and entered Jonathan's strike.

Jonathan remained where he was, observing Erin as she sat at the small desk. The small overhead lamp gleamed off her dark hair. Jonathan moved closer, fascinated by the way she nibbled at her bottom lip in apparent concentration.

Erin was aware of Jonathan's presence even before he reached out to tuck a few loose strands of her dark hair behind her left ear. In the process his index finger grazed the outer rim of her ear and lingered long enough to instigate another series of tingles. Just as she was getting suspicious about the intent of his touch, Jonathan stepped away from her and calmly said, "Your hair was getting in your way. I didn't mean to disturb you."

"You didn't disturb me. I was just checking our scores." At least her voice sounded normal, even if her pulse rate wasn't.

Jonathan moved closer, bracing his left hand on the scoring desk while resting his right hand on the back of her chair. "How am I doing?"

"Better than I expected." *In more ways than one!* she silently added.

Jonathan had to smile at her disgruntled expression. "I'm glad."

Erin wasn't. Directing Jonathan for the next eight weeks would be difficult enough. She had no intention of inviting any further complications!

CHAPTER FOUR

By the time first rehearsals began the next evening, Erin had convinced herself that her reaction to Jonathan at the bowling alley the night before had been the result of a week containing too much caffeine and too little sleep. Consequently she'd limited her coffee intake while waiting around for the rehearsal to begin.

She'd been the first to arrive at The Little Theatre, which wasn't surprising considering the fact that she was there a good hour ahead of time. She had no cause to be nervous; she'd done her homework well. *The Importance of Being Earnest* would be the third production that Erin had directed, and she'd learned a lot from her previous directing experiences.

She looked down at the artistically lettered signs she had in her hand: "In the theater the director is God—but unfortunately the actors are atheists." That one would look good on the wall directly behind her worktable, Erin decided with a grin. The next sign was a quote by Sir Ralph Richardson, which Erin had always found to be valid: "The most precious things in speech are pauses." She posted that sign right over the coffee machine, where it was sure to be noticed. She'd just applied the last bit of adhesive tape to the sign's corner when Wanda and her husband, Ned, joined her.

"Wonderful sign. You even got it straight! Look what I've brought you as a reward. Some homemade cookies," Wanda announced, waving the trayful of goodies beneath Erin's nose.

"Not your Polish grandmother's recipe for butter cookies?" Erin exclaimed with closed eyes and an expression of ecstasy.

"Is there any other kind of butter cookie?" Wanda retorted.

"I hope you realize that these cookies are single-handedly responsible for the ten pounds I gained during our last production."

"I know. It's a plot," Wanda readily admitted. "I'm going to fatten everyone by ten pounds, and then no one will notice that I've got to *lose* ten pounds."

Erin shook her head at Wanda. "Devious, very devious."

Wanda just grinned unrepentantly. "I know, I know. That's why you asked for me as your stage manager."

"That and the fact that I know I can safely leave the production in your more-than-capable hands after opening night."

Wanda had been with the Village Players for over ten years now. She'd met her husband at the theater. Ned was an electrician who'd been roped into taking care of the theater's temperamental light and sound system. After a leisurely courtship they'd been married on the Little Theatre's front lawn.

In the real world, as the theater group liked to call it, Wanda worked for the phone company, but she devoted most of her free time to the Village Players. So did Ned, without whose presence Erin knew she would have blown a fuse or two herself! He was a whiz at anything electrical or electronic.

As the starting time for the rehearsal drew nearer, people began to arrive. Dan, Paul, and Jonathan all arrived at the same time, for which Erin was grateful.

Although confident of her own abilities to cope with Jonathan, she had no desire to test those abilities immediately. So she continued her discussion with Cindy, a new member of the Village Players who played the part of Jonathan's character's young ward.

This was Cindy's first leading role, and the highschool senior was bubbling with enthusiasm and nervousness.

"I've been doing a lot of research on Oscar Wilde," Cindy stated. "I want my performance to be well rounded, and to do that I feel I need to know where the playwright is coming from."

"Wilde came from Ireland," Artie inserted with typical humor. The owner of a used-car dealership, Artie always had a twinkle in his eyes and a quip on his tongue. He often said the combination was the secret to his enjoyment of life at sixty-five. Artie was another long-term member of the Village Players, and Erin had worked with him before. He would be acting the part of the village vicar.

As soon as everyone was assembled, Erin formally opened the play's first rehearsal. "Tonight we'll be doing a read-through of the entire play." Wanda began handing out scripts while Erin was speaking. "I don't want you worrying about memorizing your lines now," Erin went on to say for the benefit of those new to acting. "This reading is meant to make everyone familiar with all the characters in the play and their reactions to one another. It's easier to get a fix on things if you hear each character's lines read aloud by that character rather than reciting the entire thing in your head. It's also a chance to hear the entire play at one time because during upcoming rehearsals we'll only be rehearsing one scene or act at a time."

For the next hour and a half the nine characters read their lines, stopping in between the first and second acts for a coffee break.

Everyone welcomed the opportunity to "wet their

whistle," as Artie put it. Erin stuck to decaffeinated coffee and tried to limit herself to three of Wanda's habit-forming cookies.

"So how'd it go the other night?" Dan asked Erin as he poured himself a cup of coffee. Seeing her blank look, he elaborated further. "You and Jonathan."

"We went bowling."

"I know. I was right next to you when you offered to teach him how to have fun, remember?"

"I'll take your word for it," Erin returned.

"So how did it go?"

"Okay."

"That's it? Only okay?"

Erin fixed him with a reprimanding stare. "Dan, I hate to tell you this, but you're beginning to sound like a match-maker. Now, I know that couldn't actually be the case, because I know how much you dislike matchmaking yourself. Why, I remember the time Wanda set you up with her cousin Hannah—"

"All right, I get the message," Dan hurriedly interrupted. Disconcerted, he looked around to make sure no one had overheard them. "Say no more."

"I won't if you won't," Erin promised.

"You won't what?" Jonathan asked from directly behind her.

"Didn't anyone ever tell you that it's rude to sneak up on people?" Erin demanded as she grabbed a paper napkin and dabbed at the coffee she'd sloshed over her hand.

"Sneaking involves a degree of clandestineness and fur-tiveness that was not present in my approach," Jonathan re-plied with legal precision.

"Trying to blind us with big words, counselor?" Erin taunted.

"I wouldn't dream of it," Jonathan said in denial as he reached around Erin to take one of Wanda's cookies.

"I suppose I should have told you that rehearsals are casual, Jonathan," Erin told him. "We really don't require formal attire."

"Who's formal?" Jonathan asked, looking around as if in search of the culprit.

"You are."

"No, I'm not. Formal attire means a tux and bow tie. I'm merely wearing a suit."

"The only person wearing a suit," Erin pointed out. "It's safe here, you're among friends. Right, Dan?"

Dan almost choked on the cookie he was eating. "Uh, right."

"Then please tell your friend that he doesn't have to wear a suit to rehearsals."

"You don't have to wear a suit to rehearsals," Dan obediently repeated.

"I know that."

"He knows that," Dan relayed.

"I wear a suit out of choice."

"He wears a suit out of—"

"I heard him, Dan," Erin interrupted. "I'm just finding it hard to believe him."

Luckily the lenses of Jonathan's glasses hid the momentary flash of alarm that lit his eyes.

"I mean, who would prefer to wear a suit when given a choice?" Erin went on to ask rhetorically.

Jonathan drew in a sigh of relief. For a moment there, he thought she'd found him out. "Does this mean I need more help in the *joie-de-vivre* department?" he innocently inquired.

"Judging by your clothes, I'd say you do. Could you at

least make the effort to dress more casually?" Erin requested.

Jonathan had a hard time keeping a straight face in light of Erin's long-suffering expression. "I'll do the best I can."

"I guess that's the most I can hope for." Erin sighed and moved on.

You're the most I could hope for, Jonathan thought to himself as he watched Erin walk away. She wore a pair of red slacks that fit her just right. Jonathan found himself grinning as he appreciated the view. Red just might become his favorite color from now on.

When the rehearsal ended, Jonathan stayed behind in order to speak to Erin. "You never told me when you'd scheduled lesson two."

"Lesson two?" It took Erin a moment to realize what he was talking about. "Oh, right, lesson two."

"How about dinner this time?" Jonathan suggested before she could come up with something wild. While he'd enjoyed bowling with her, the ambience hadn't exactly been conducive to seduction. A candlelit dinner was more in line with his intentions.

Erin, however, was still taking her job as teacher seriously and had no such romantic visions. "You want to broaden your tastes in food, you mean? I suppose I could manage that, so long as you're willing to experiment with something a little more exotic than steak and potatoes and let me choose the restaurant."

Wondering what he was letting himself in for, Jonathan reluctantly agreed. "All right. When?"

They set a date and a time that was mutually agreeable, and Erin gave Jonathan directions to her gatehouse. Apparently he had no trouble with the map she'd drawn him, because he arrived precisely on time Sunday night. Erin wasn't ready yet, not that it was her fault. Butch had claimed squatter's rights on the dress she'd set out to wear after her bath and she'd had to change her outfit when the hefty feline showed no signs of moving. The baggy trousers she chose as a replacement resembled harem pants and had a loose waistband. That was an important consideration when eating at the Four Seasons. The food was always plentiful and superb.

"I'm coming," Erin hollered as the brass door knocker was rapped again. "Be there in a sec!" She buttoned the last button of her blouse and hurriedly jammed the silk material into her cinnamon-colored slacks. Her shoes would have to wait.

The first thing Erin said after opening the door was, "Couldn't you have been a little late?"

Not the most auspicious way to begin an evening, Jonathan admitted to himself with a wry grimace. "Shall I come back and we'll start over again?"

"No." Erin grabbed his arm and tugged him inside. "It's not your fault, it's Butch's."

"And who, may I ask, is Butch?"

"He's right over there." Erin pointed to the large tomcat, who now was sitting on the window seat of the bay window on the opposite side of the room.

"Nice kitty," Jonathan murmured encouragingly.

"He hates to be called kitty," Erin told Jonathan. "Just turn on the TV. I think there's a football game on tonight and he loves football. I'll be right back."

"Football! You're kidding, right?" But Erin had already left the room.

Butch, meanwhile, was eyeing Jonathan with a flinty stare.

"You act like this with all the guys Erin goes out with or just me?" Jonathan asked the cat.

Butch froze. His whiskers were the only thing moving, and they twitched—an ominous sign.

"I was only kidding," Jonathan murmured as he made his way to the couch, which was conveniently placed as far away from the cat as the confines of the room allowed.

Jonathan had barely seated himself when Butch made his move. Like a guided missile, the cat launched himself across the room, directly at Jonathan!

Erin returned to the living room just in time to see Jonathan's reflexive start. By the time she said, "Don't worry," Butch was already half perched on Jonathan's shoulder.

"Butch isn't after you, he's after the fly on the wall behind you," Erin explained in a reassuring voice.

Sure enough, Butch consumed the fly in one fell swoop.

"Don't you ever feed your cat?" Jonathan demanded with a shudder.

"Flies are a great delicacy," she retorted.

With one final satisfied lick of his chops, Butch jumped off Jonathan's shoulder onto the floor, where he proceeded to wash himself in the center of the rug.

"Would you like a drink before we leave?" Erin asked Jonathan, as if nothing untoward had occurred.

"After that performance?" Jonathan shook his head. "No, thanks. I'll pass."

Erin shrugged. "Your choice." She wrapped a hand-woven shawl around her shoulders. "I'm ready to leave if you are."

The Four Seasons restaurant was not located in the best section of Portland, and it didn't have a lovely view of any of the city's scenic sights, such as the snowy peak of Mt. Hood, or the Willamette and Columbia Rivers. In fact, it didn't appear to have any windows at all. Even its front door was unusual.

"You're sure there's a restaurant in here?" Jonathan questioned as Erin pushed the small door bell located to the side of the closed door.

"Positive. See, here's the sign." She pointed to a tiny brass plate that read FOUR SEASONS in tarnished letters.

Before Jonathan could voice his skepticism, a heretofore hidden speakeasy door slid open, revealing a pair of eyes.

"Grigor! How are you?"

Jonathan had no idea how Erin could identify someone by that brief glimpse of a pair of eyes, and he told her so. "How do you know it's Grigor?"

"Everyone knows Grigor," Erin retorted as the small trapdoor slid shut.

As a series of dead-bolt locks and other magical mechanisms were undone, Jonathan sardonically murmured, "What is this, Fort Knox?"

"Grigor's guarding something better than gold."

Jonathan wasn't sure he liked the sound of that. What had he gotten himself in for?

"And stop looking so suspicious," Erin hissed right before the door was opened. "This is a family-style restaurant, not an opium den. You're lucky to be let in, especially since you're wearing a suit."

The world on the other side of the door was far removed from the deceptively deserted hallway from which they'd just come. Jonathan felt as if he'd stepped onto a movie set for *The Arabian Nights*. Material was draped from the ceiling, giving the impression of a tent. The place was packed with people. Long wooden tables were set up and piled with exotic-smelling food. Wooden benches were provided for seating, which appeared to be at a premium.

While Jonathan was taking note of his surroundings Grigor was hugging Erin and kissing her on each cheek. "Welcome! Welcome! Come, sit and eat."

Grigor shooed two dawdling customers out of their seats and put Erin and Jonathan in their places.

"We have fetayer, sujuq, and maqanek to start." As he was speaking Grigor waved a waitress over to them. She set down three dishes full of food. Erin handed Jonathan an empty plate from a pile in the center of the table.

"I must get back to the kitchen," Grigor said. "Enjoy! Later we will have music and dancing."

"Where's the menu?" Jonathan asked.

"There is no menu. I told you, it's family-style."

"Howard Johnson's is family-style, and they have a menu."

"Here family-style refers to the fact that you are served whatever Grigor has decided to cook, as if you were coming to his home to eat. But you're lucky. Tonight you've got a choice of either sojuq or maqanek. You'll probably want the maqanek, that's milder than the sujuq."

"I'm not eating anything until I know what it is."

"Armenian sausage."

"Oh."

"And this is fatayer." Erin pointed to the third dish. "It's chopped spinach, onion, and pine nuts in pastry dough."

"Pine nuts?"

"It's very good. Have some."

Surprisingly it was good, and Jonathan enjoyed the appetizers as much as he did the main course of shish kebab. The charbroiled bits of lamb, green peppers, onions, and tomatoes were done to perfection. Jonathan was not accustomed to eating shish kebab with his fingers, however.

"It's a house rule," Erin told Jonathan as she tucked a napkin into his shirt collar. "Newcomers have to eat with their fingers. It's a sign to the chief, Grigor, that you find his cooking finger-lickin' good."

"You'd better show me how it's done," Jonathan suggested.

Erin obligingly tugged a morsel of lamb from the skewer and held it up to Jonathan's lips. "Open," she instructed him.

As his lips brushed her fingers Erin again fell prey to sensual currents of pleasure. Frowning, she removed her fingers from temptation and stared at them. She then studied Jonathan, who was contentedly munching the food she'd just given him.

"Mmmm, good," he murmured.

"You can help yourself," Erin said.

"I plan to," Jonathan assured her in a deceptively soft voice.

She had difficulty untangling her gaze from his. Was it a trick of the lighting or was Jonathan looking at her as if she were the meal he was about to consume? Erin blinked and checked his expression again. Nothing. She must have imagined it.

Jonathan was hard-pressed to restrain a grin. He knew Erin was confused by her reaction to him. He also knew that she'd caught the look he'd just given her. He'd only allowed her a brief, tantalizing glimpse of his hunger for her. Jonathan had never been a hunter, but Erin certainly did bring out the tracker instincts in him. She also brought out a lot of other, baser instincts in him! She'd no doubt be quite stunned if she knew the erotic plans for her that her supposed stuffed-shirt student was harboring at the moment. Jonathan even surprised himself. He'd never wanted a woman this much before.

The after-dinner entertainment of belly dancing didn't help ease his desire any. Instead of focusing on the dark-haired beauty performing the Middle Eastern dance, Jonathan found himself imagining Erin with a jewel in her navel and little else on in the way of clothing. It didn't help his restraint to have Grigor stop by their table after the performance and inform him that Erin did indeed know how to belly dance.

"My wife says that Erin is her best pupil. You must get Erin to dance for you," Grigor stated.

"I'll work on it," Jonathan promised.

"So you're a belly dancer, director, actress, and graphic artist," Jonathan said as he drove her home. "Is there anything else about you that I should know?"

"No."

"You don't talk about your work much, do you?"

"Neither do you," she pointed out.

"That's true, but then, I doubt that my work is as interesting as yours."

"Actually things are kind of tense at the office right now," she admitted. "So as soon as I leave, I close the door on my problems at work."

"Sounds like a good philosophy. I tend to do the same thing myself."

"You do?"

Jonathan nodded. "See, we do have something in common."

"I never said we didn't."

"How do you think my lessons are progressing?"

She sent him a teasing look. "They're going fairly well considering the handicap I'm working under."

"Handicap?"

"You may be acting more laid-back, but you're still dressing like a tax attorney. I'm dying to hear what your excuse is today. It's Sunday, you know. Even tax attorneys must have Sundays off."

"We do."

"Then why are you still wearing a suit?"

"This is my Sunday suit. It's gray instead of dark blue. And my shirt is blue instead of white."

"You're still a long way from casual," Erin told him.

"But I'm not a long way from your house. Here we are." Jonathan pulled his car to a stop behind Erin's Voyager mini-van. He got out and walked around the front of the car to open the passenger door for Erin. She had to confess to being pleased at the small courtesy.

When they reached her front door, Erin fully expected Jonathan to kiss her. She was prepared for his kiss and Jonathan knew it. Which is why he politely shook her hand instead.

"Thank you for introducing me to the wonders of Armenian cooking."

"You're welcome," Erin murmured in a slightly bewildered voice.

Jonathan released her hand. "Good night."

"Good night."

Erin slipped her key into the dead-bolt lock and told herself that she was relieved Jonathan hadn't kissed her. Their relationship, if it could even be called such, was not romantic. As she brushed her teeth she was still telling herself the same thing. It didn't do a lot of good. She continued to feel slightly off-balance, and she didn't like the feeling. What's more, Jonathan refused to leave her thoughts. He even appeared in her dreams.

Which was exactly what he'd intended, of course. Jonathan knew the only way to slip beneath Erin's defenses was to catch her unprepared, which he did during a rehearsal a few days later.

Erin was blocking Act One. Wanda had marked out the confines of the stage door with colored tape, indicating where the various openings were through which the players would be making their exits and entrances. Metal chairs and wooden tables had been placed on stage as stand-ins for the furniture of the final set, which Dan was still collecting.

Only those actors whose characters made an appearance in Act One were present for this first walkthrough. At this point Erin was concerned about the scene's visual impression. Was the action clear? Seeing the actors moving around gave her a visual basis for correcting her blocking.

Things were progressing slowly but steadily until they reached the scene involving Sue as Gwendolen and Jonathan was John Worthing alias Ernest. "You're supposed to be in love with Gwendolen," Erin reminded Jonathan. "You shouldn't be sitting ten feet away from her. You're supposed to embrace her. She's just told you she loves you. . . . No, no, that's not right," Erin complained after Jonathan and Sue tried it again.

"Maybe it would help if you came and showed me exactly what it is you're looking for in this scene," Jonathan smoothly suggested.

"Fine." Erin tossed her prompt book to Wanda and took Sue's place beside Jonathan. "You sit down beside Gwendolen on what will be a love seat, and you say your line."

Jonathan did so. " 'Darling! You don't know how happy you've made me.' " But you soon will, he thought to himself as he set up his next move.

"That's better. Now Sue says, 'My darling Ernest,' and the two of you embrace, like this." Erin slipped her arms around Jonathan's waist and was surprised to feel his arms slip around her with smooth precision. Confidently tugging her closer, he murmured, "Like this?" before swooping down to kiss her.

CHAPTER FIVE

Like this? Erin's mind dazedly repeated Jonathan's question. Yes, she did like it—very much.

His mouth was warm and commanding. Coaxing her lips apart, Jonathan skillfully developed the kiss into an increasingly intimate caress. He drew her further into the arena of excitement by nibbling on the delicate softness of her lower lip until Erin was seduced by shivers of pleasure. Her startled moan provided the basis for his next assault as his mouth moved over hers with persuasive intent.

His tongue began a series of enticing moves that soon had her tongue greeting his with equal abandon. He savored her taste as a connoisseur might savor a fine wine. The pacing slowed. Where before he'd taken her by storm, now he paused to dally and explore.

The kiss was so all-consuming that Erin forgot her surroundings, forgot everything. Intent on prolonging the pleasure, she slipped her hands from his waist up to the nape of his neck where she sank her fingers into his dark hair and guided him even closer. Jonathan responded by deepening the kiss and shifting her in his arms so that they were pressed together from shoulder to thigh. She could feel the pounding of his heart, or was it her own? Through the momentary fog clouding Erin's mind she suddenly heard the sound of muted laughter.

"Okay, you two, break it up. We get the idea!" Martha exclaimed in the resounding voice that years of theatrical experience had given her.

As if stung, Erin jerked away from Jonathan and raggedly inhaled the air so needed by her oxygen-starved lungs. Her voice and her fighting spirit restored, she got to her feet and regally announced, "That's how it should be done."

The other members of the company applauded appreciatively.

Jonathan, meanwhile, hadn't even steamed up his glasses! His lips did bear the mark of her watermelon-red lipstick, however. Erin noted that fact with some degree of triumph. He hadn't escaped entirely unscathed after all.

"That wraps up tonight's rehearsals, folks," Erin announced. "See you all here Saturday afternoon at one."

"Wow! That was some performance," Wanda exclaimed as she returned the director's prompt book to Erin.

Erin looked at the lines of print and wondered why they made no sense. Then she realized that she was holding the book upside down. She turned it right side up again, wishing she could do the same with her own perspective. She felt upside down and inside out.

"Are you joining us at the pub?" Martha asked Erin. It was traditional for everyone to stop at the Lion's Inn Pub after rehearsals to talk about the play and how it was progressing.

"I'll be there," Erin promised, because, if she hadn't, everyone might guess that she wasn't as calm as she appeared to be.

Thankfully Jonathan stayed out of her way until Erin arrived at the pub. The ten-minute drive from the Little Theatre hadn't been long enough for her to get her thoughts in order. The logical, sensible thing to do would be to forget Jonathan's kiss. The only problem was that Erin rarely did the logical or sensible thing, and she found it impossible to forget the kiss.

She told herself that putting on a play was an extremely in-

Cathie Linz

tense yet equally artificial situation. She'd seen trouble develop before during theatrical productions. Romances sprang from all the late-night rehearsal activity, the constant proximity. And she'd seen those relationships wither once the play closed.

Which was why Erin had made it a point never to get romantically involved with anyone from the theater group. Instead they had all become members of her adopted family. But Jonathan refused to fit that mold. In fact, he didn't fit a lot of molds. Where had a stuffed-shirt tax attorney learned to kiss like that? Not by reading the IRS Handbook or whatever it was called, that's for sure!

Once inside the pub, Erin ordered a Perrier with a twist of lime for herself. She needed to keep her wits about her, and tempting though the thought of consuming an entire carafe of white wine might sound, the after-effects were more than likely only to get her deeper into trouble.

To her surprise Jonathan was drinking a soft drink instead of his usual bottle of imported beer.

"Great minds," he murmured, nodding at the nonalcoholic drink in her hand.

"We may both have great minds," she retorted, "but we don't think at all alike."

"Maybe we should sit down and compare notes," he softly suggested.

"Maybe we should sit down and join the others." Erin was pleased at how lightly she tossed back the mocking comment.

Her idea didn't seem so bright, however, when Jonathan sat beside her. Whenever she moved, he moved. His shoulder brushed her shoulder, his knee touched her knee.

"Listen, Erin, I've got a problem . . ." Dan began.

So have I, Erin thought to herself with a dark glare in Jonathan's direction. *And he's sitting right next to me!*

Unaware of her thoughts, Dan went on with his speech. "You remember I told you that I'd have to be out of town this Saturday, so I'll miss tomorrow's rehearsal."

"I remember."

"Well, there's another complication to consider now."

Doesn't surprise me, Erin thought to herself with a frown. Complications seemed to be abounding lately.

"Erin, are you listening to me?" Dan demanded.

"I'm listening."

"All right, then. You remember Mrs. Durkee?"

"Mrs. Durkee? The local pack rat?"

Dan nodded. "She's the one. You know I've been trying to gain entrance to her famed attic for the last two months, right?"

"Right. So?"

"So, she's finally decided to allow me to check her attic for those few props we still need. The catch is that tomorrow is the only day she'll allow me in."

"That is a problem."

"Not if you'd agree to go in my place," Dan suggested.

"How would Mrs. Durkee feel about that?" Erin asked.

"She doesn't mind. I already checked."

"How foresighted of you." Erin's voice was tinged with disgruntled humor.

"Isn't it, though?" Dan agreed with a smile. "So? Will you go in my place?"

"All right. Just give me a list of what it is I'm looking for."

"I've got the list right here." Dan pulled a folded piece of paper from his pocket.

"It's a good thing I've got my van to haul all this stuff," Erin wryly noted as she took the list from Dan.

"It's also a good thing you've got me to help you load it,"

Jonathan inserted.

Erin declined the offer. "Thanks, but I won't need any help."

Jonathan didn't look at all put out by her refusal.

"Too bad. You've got me whether you want me or not."

That was the problem, Erin glumly decided as she watched Dan and Jonathan tie up the final arrangements. She wanted Jonathan entirely too much. *So what are you going to do about it?* she asked herself.

Unfortunately she was no closer to finding an answer to that all-important question when she pulled up in front of Mrs. Durkee's four-story Victorian home the next morning. As prearranged, Jonathan was already parked at the curb, waiting for Erin.

The first thing she noticed about him was that he wasn't wearing a suit, but his charcoal-gray trousers, white shirt, and navy sweater weren't exactly casual, either. Especially since he was wearing a tie. "You're getting closer," she told him, "but you don't quite have it down pat yet. Don't you have any grubby clothes that you could have worn? After all, we will be scrounging around in a dusty old attic."

"Had you invited me to your place for breakfast, you could have coached me on the proper attire for attic scrounging."

"What?" Erin's eyes widened with mocking astonishment. "And force you to face Butch again?"

Jonathan dismissed her words with a knightly wave of his hand. "What's a mere tomcat compared to the gauntlet of bowling alleys and Armenian restaurants you've already put me through?"

"Hey, consider yourself lucky. Instead of bowling, I could have taken you ice skating at the Lloyd Center, or hiking on the rim of Portland's own extinct volcano, Mount Tabor."

Seeing his expression of surprise, Erin said, "You mean, you've lived in Portland for all of . . ." She paused to allow him to fill in the blank.

"Twenty months."

". . . and you never knew we have an extinct volcano?" She shook her head. "It's amazing how blind people are to their own environment."

"That's why I wear glasses," Jonathan retorted with droll amusement as Erin tugged on the old-fashioned bellpull gracing Mrs. Durkee's front porch.

The first few chords of "London Bridge Is Falling Down" precluded Erin's having to make a response.

"Ah, there you are, dears." The seventy-two-year-old lady who'd opened the door looked like something right out of the movie *Arsenic and Old Lace.* But the gleam in Mrs. Durkee's eyes showed that she wasn't as frail as she appeared to be.

"Mrs. Durkee, I'm Erin Rossi, and this is Jonathan Garrett. We're with the Village Players. You said it would be okay for us to come over today to look through your attic for props."

Holding open the screen door, the elderly woman invited them both into her home. "Would you like some lemonade first? I made some fresh this morning."

Erin shook her head. "You don't need to bother. . . ."

"It's no bother," Mrs. Durkee insisted, pointing them into the front parlor. "Sit, sit, both of you. Would you mind pouring, dear?" the elderly woman asked Erin. "My hands aren't as steady as they used to be, and I wouldn't want to spill any on the carpet."

Erin poured out three tall glasses of lemonade and handed one each to Jonathan and Mrs. Durkee.

"So. How long have you and this young man known each other?" Mrs. Durkee gregariously asked Erin.

"Not very long," Erin replied in what was meant to be a dismissive voice.

Mrs. Durkee didn't take the hint. "Sometimes it doesn't take long to know you've met the right one. I knew as soon as I laid eyes on my Ralph. Something inside of me just . . . tingled."

"More lemonade?" Erin asked rather desperately. She didn't want to hear about tingles. They came too close to describing what she'd experienced with Jonathan.

"No, thank you, dear, but you help yourself if you'd like some more. There's plenty in the pitcher. Now . . . where was I? Oh, yes. I was talking about that special tingle I got when I first saw Ralph."

Not one to give up easily, Erin tried changing the subject again. "This is a lovely house, Mrs. Durkee. Have you lived here long?"

"Don't interrupt," Jonathan reprimanded Erin. "Mrs. Durkee is telling us about Ralph."

And so Erin had to sit through a half-hour reminiscence of how Mrs. Durkee fell in love with her Ralph. "But you young people didn't come here to listen to my stories," she concluded with a smile. "You came to look through the attic for some things for your play, isn't that correct?"

Erin nodded.

"Well go on up, then," Mrs. Durkee instructed them. "It's all the way at the top of the third flight of stairs. I feel like I've forgotten something, isn't that strange?" Mrs. Durkee paused to think for a moment. "It's gone right out of my head now. Never mind. It couldn't have been important."

"The top of the third flight of stairs, you said?" Erin questioned.

"That's right, dear. You can't miss it. Take anything you need. It all should be thrown away, but I haven't got the heart to do it. This way at least I know it will be going to a good home. I'll wait for you down here."

"Aren't you glad I came along to help you carry things?" Jonathan demanded as they made their way up the second long flight of stairs.

Erin avoided answering his question by asking one of her own. "How many rooms do you think there are in this house?"

"More to the point, how many stairs are there? Ah, here we are. This must be the door to the attic."

"It could be, but I can't tell, it's so dark." Erin dug a small flashlight out of her purse and flicked it on. "There should be a light switch in here somewhere. Aha! Found it." She flicked on the switch and the dusty attic was immediately illuminated by a bare bulb affixed to the rafters.

"Okay, let's get to work. According to Dan's list we're looking for . . ." Erin rattled off several different objects, including a love seat, a cigarette or cigar case, and a black leather bag.

"A love seat?"

"A piece of furniture that looks like a couch without any back, and it's got a sort of back where you'd expect an arm to be," Erin explained.

"Whose arm?" Jonathan asked. "Yours or mine?"

"Very funny. Here, you take Dan's list and check that side of the attic. I'll take this side."

Erin was efficiently sorting through piles of junk and setting aside a few things they needed, when she suddenly found herself face-to-face with a giant beast with bared teeth. Her startled scream brought Jonathan to her side in an instant.

His hands cupped her elbows as he drew her to him and anxiously demanded, "What is it?"

"You tell me." She pointed a slightly unsteady finger in the beast's direction.

Jonathan turned to stare at the unsightly apparition. "It's a bear."

"Gross!" Erin shuddered.

"He's really in no shape to be bothering anyone," Jonathan assured her.

"Fine. Since you feel that way, you can take this side, and I'll go work on the other side."

"Fine by me," Jonathan agreed. He waited until she was on the opposite section of the attic before adding, "Watch out for the moose head, though."

"What! Where?"

"There, about ten feet to your left."

"At least it doesn't have teeth," Erin muttered.

"Let's hope it doesn't have fleas, either."

"Thank you for those words of reassurance, counselor."

Jonathan gave her a mocking salute. "Anytime."

"You now have a smear of dust across your forehead," Erin said, taking great glee in informing him. "No, don't bother wiping it off," she said as he automatically raised his hand on a cleanup mission. "I think it helps soften your corporate look. Besides, you're sure to add more dirt to that before our search is over."

Jonathan shrugged and lowered his hand. "You're probably right. Which is why I've courteously refrained from telling you about the smudge on your nose."

Erin wrinkled her dusty nose at him before resuming her search. The attic was a cleaner's nightmare, but it was a collector's dream. Erin found an old wind-up Victrola and a stack of records that she would have loved to go through, had there been time.

Awhile later she came across an oak hat stand filled with

hats. There was one drooping Edwardian picture hat with faded silk flowers that particularly caught Erin's eye. It called out to her, tempting her to try it on. She'd seen a mirror earlier behind that pile of boxes to her right. Sneaking a peek at Jonathan to make sure he wasn't looking, Erin grabbed the hat and ducked out of sight.

There was barely enough light to see and the mirror was speckled with age, but Erin was as excited as a little girl as she carefully placed the hat on her head and tied the wide ribbons into a bow beneath her chin.

"Hey, look what I found!" Jonathan exclaimed from the other side of the boxes. "Erin? Where are you?"

"Stay there, I'll be there in a second!" Her fingers were all thumbs as she unsuccessfully attempted to undo the bow, which had somehow transformed itself into a stubborn knot. Erin looked up into the mirror and found Jonathan's reflection right behind hers.

"Having problems?" he inquired with a slight smile.

"Nothing I can't handle."

His voice was husky as he said, "Mmmm, but why bother when I'd much rather handle it for you?" True to his words, Jonathan reached out to untie the knot for her. His fingers brushed against the sensitive skin beneath her chin, instigating a chain reaction of pleasurable sensations that soon had her trembling.

Gazing down at her face, Jonathan couldn't resist the lure of her unique beauty. He kissed her mouth, and then her cheek and chin. Her lips parted as she breathed his name— half in protest, half in invitation.

Jonathan's fingers finally mastered the knot and ever so slowly slid one entwined ribbon through the other. The satiny friction against Erin's already hypersensitive skin proved to be her undoing. Almost swaying with need, she met his wandering lips with blatant hunger.

Jonathan, however, continued his tantalizing ways. Instead of lavishing her with his tongue, he barely parted his lips. Temptingly he brushed his mouth across hers—back and forth in a rhythm that Erin found intoxicating.

She didn't even realize that she'd moved with him until she felt him urging her down. "Don't worry. I found the love seat."

A moment later Erin felt the solidity of a piece of furniture beneath her as Jonathan smoothly urged her into a reclining position. "I don't think you'll need this anymore," he whispered in a husky voice as he swept the hat from her head.

The small deed brought Erin to her senses more abruptly than a pail of cold water could have done. She was no Edwardian lady falling into a swoon in a man's arms. She was a modern woman with serious reservations about the wisdom of getting involved with Jonathan. "What are you doing?" she demanded as much of herself as of him.

Jonathan frowned at her abrupt reversal. "What does it feel like I'm doing?"

"Trying to seduce me, and you can forget it!" Placing both hands palm down on his chest, she shoved him away from her. "Teaching you how to have a good time does not include lessons on the intimacies of lovemaking!" Not that he appeared to need any lessons in that department!

"Erin, you don't understand . . . ."

"I understand exactly." She grabbed the hat and stomped off with it. "There." She plunked the hat back where she'd found it. "Fantasy time is over. Now, let's get back to work. We still need a black leather bag. It plays a critical part in the dramatic resolution of the last act."

Correctly suspecting that Erin was in no mood to listen to reason, Jonathan decided not to argue with her decision for the time being. But he had no intention of letting the matter rest indefinitely. He and Erin were going to have a little talk before the day was over, whether she was willing or not.

Determined to end this search quickly, Erin methodically sorted through piles of odds and ends until she found a leather bag that would fit the bill perfectly. Now they could leave.

"We'll save the love seat for last," Erin decided with a glare at that piece of furniture, as if it were partly responsible for her brief lapse of control. "We can carry the small things down first."

"There's just one problem," Jonathan announced from his position near the attic door. "It appears that we're locked in here."

"You must be mistaken!" Erin hurriedly dropped what she was carrying on the love seat and joined Jonathan at the door. The doorknob turned, but the door remained firmly closed.

To make matters even worse, the lone light bulb chose that moment to go out, throwing the attic into darkness.

CHAPTER SIX

Jonathan made the most of the situation by taking Erin in his arms and telling her not to panic.

"I'm not going to panic," Erin retorted, "but I can't breathe when you hold me this tightly." She was bending the truth a bit. While it was true that she did feel breathless, the cause was the sheer temptation of Jonathan's embrace and not the tightness of his grip.

"I can't breathe, either," Jonathan muttered in her ear. "You have that effect on me. So what are we going to do about it?"

Surprised by his question, she sputtered, "I . . ."

"Sounds good to me," he growled before capturing her mouth in a kiss. His aim was remarkably accurate considering the darkness. His lips merged with hers—parting them, devouring them.

Erin didn't even go through the motions of protesting. Her desire for Jonathan had finally reached the point where it superseded her desire to play it safe. Feeling as if she were giving in to the inevitable, she responded with a hunger that matched his. One kiss blended into another as they explored tastes and textures.

Jonathan drew her closer. His hands slid beneath her knit cotton top, beneath her silk chemise, and glided up her bare back, skimming the dips and ridges of her spine. Excitement shivered over her skin as his hands caressed her.

When he first touched her breasts, she caught her breath. His palm cupped her while his supple fingers worked their magic. Images of forbidden pleasures superimposed themselves on her mind, prompting her to assuage her curiosity about the lean male body pressed so tightly against her own.

Slipping her hands beneath his sweater, she tugged his shirt from his slacks and proceeded to let her hands roam freely across the firm expanse of his back. Jonathan feathered a series of kisses across her face to her ear, where he whispered words of encouragement. Erin was more than happy to oblige, wiggling closer and standing on tiptoe to work on unfastening his tie. She didn't even realize that he'd removed his glasses until she felt him nuzzling the base of her throat.

Her husky purr of approval rippled its way through him. Well aware of the tautening of his body, Erin leaned into him. Jonathan widened his stance slightly until his legs closed around hers. Urging her up to him, he lifted her until she was half perched upon his bracing thigh. With skillful precision he then slowly let her slide back down his leg, only to draw her up once again. The erotic friction soon had her giddy with pleasure.

She was fluid and feverish, twisting in his arms to find some measure of satisfaction for the aching desire growing within her.

"That's it, honey." He was in the process of shifting his hold on her when an ominous crack sounded nearby, followed immediately thereafter by the sound of Jonathan's muffled curse.

Erin found herself abruptly released and standing on her own. She stumbled slightly before regaining her footing. "What's wrong?" Her voice was husky with passion and bewilderment.

"I just hit my elbow on a beam," Jonathan muttered in disgust.

Concerned, she asked, "Are you all right?"

"No. My arm's numb and the rest of me is—"

"I already know how the rest of you is," Erin interrupted with a seductive smile that could be heard in her voice, even if it couldn't be seen in the darkness.

"Then you also know the cure for my . . . pressing . . . condition. Unfortunately this attic is obviously not the place for such activities. But as soon as we get out of here . . ."

"We have a rehearsal to go to," Erin reminded him.

"Damn! I forgot all about it." Jonathan slipped his glasses back on and pressed the illuminating bar on his watch. "It's almost twelve-thirty already."

Erin groaned. "I didn't know it was that late. We've got to get out of here."

"Where's your flashlight?" Jonathan questioned.

"In my back pocket."

"I thought I felt something odd," he murmured wryly.

"Cute." In retribution Erin aimed the flashlight at Jonathan's face. She was oddly disappointed to find that he'd put his glasses back on. "Very cute. Now, what do you suggest we do?"

"Let's see if we can get Mrs. Durkee's attention."

Their yells and pounding on the door and door proved to be unsuccessful.

"Any more bright ideas?" Erin demanded in a voice hoarse from shouting.

"Let me have the flashlight a minute. I thought I saw a toolbox somewhere around here . . . there it is. And we're in luck. There's a hammer and a screwdriver in here."

Erin frowned in confusion. "What are we going to do with those?"

"Take the hinges off the door."

"Isn't that rather drastic?"

"Would you rather stay locked in here?"

"No."

"Then we don't have much choice. Here, hold the flashlight for me. I won't be doing any permanent damage," he assured her. "The door can easily be rehung."

Erin was surprised at the experienced way in which he worked with the tools. "Have you ever done this before?"

"Yes."

"When?"

"In law school."

"Oh? Was carpentry a prerequisite?"

"Not exactly. Let's just say that the ability to get yourself out of a tight situation was beneficial."

"Vaguely spoken, like a true lawyer," Erin grumbled.

"It would help if you could keep the light steady, Erin."

"My hands are unsteady because I'm hungry."

"So am I." Jonathan looked at her over his shoulder. His gaze fully qualified as a leer. "I'm absolutely starving."

"Not now, counselor." Erin shot him a sassy smile that was completely at odds with her reprimanding tone of voice. "Remember your elbow!"

Ten minutes later Jonathan had the door off its hinges and leaning up against the wall. "We're lucky that the hinges were on this side of the door or we would've been in trouble."

"We still may be in trouble when Mrs. Durkee sees what you've done to her door."

"No problem. I'll tell her we had to remove the door in order to move the love seat. Now that I think about it, that excuse is true."

They met Mrs. Durkee on the first floor landing. "Oh, there you are!" the elderly woman exclaimed. "I was getting worried. You see, I finally remembered what it was I'd forgotten to tell you. You mustn't close the attic door after you or you'll be locked inside."

Jonathan and Erin exchanged a humorous look.

"Did you find what you were looking for?" Mrs. Durkee asked them.

"We found *more* than we were looking for," Jonathan replied in a voice that relayed unspoken messages to Erin.

"Would you mind if we came back later, Mrs. Durkee, to pick up the love seat we found?" Erin asked. "We've got a rehearsal to get to and we're running a bit late."

Erin made the arrangements with Mrs. Durkee as Jonathan carried the smaller props downstairs and loaded them in Erin's van.

"Thanks again, Mrs. Durkee," Erin said as she left.

"I hope you two enjoyed the attic," Mrs. Durkee replied with a gleam in her eye. "Ralph and I always did."

Jonathan was waiting for Erin beside the van. He already had the driver's door opened for her. After helping her inside and closing the door, he leaned through the open window and gave her a brief but passionate kiss.

"See you at rehearsals."

"Jonathan." She stopped his retreat by grabbing hold of his tie, which he'd omitted to smooth back beneath his sweater after Erin had unfastened it. "Remember that we're doing an Oscar Wilde play, not something for the Playboy cable network, so watch yourself around Sue."

He blinked at her in pretended surprise. "Does that mean I'm not supposed to kiss her the way I kissed you at rehearsal yesterday?"

"That's absolutely correct."

"I suppose that also means I'm not supposed to hold her the way I held you up in the attic."

"You catch on fast," she said, congratulating him.

"I told you I'd be a good student. Wait until you see my final exam."

"I can hardly wait," she said in a breathy voice.

"Keep looking at me like that and you won't have to wait. We'll just go in the back of your van and pick up where we left off."

"And miss a rehearsal?" Erin released her hold on him. "Not allowed! See you at the theater. Last one there is a rotten egg."

Jonathan made no attempt to keep up with Erin's frantic driving pace. Instead he kept to the speed limit and carefully plotted his next move in the seduction of Erin Rossi.

The rehearsal began on time. Although Cindy didn't appear in Act One, she was attending the rehearsal because she wanted to learn as much as possible. Sensing the teenager's nervousness, Erin made it a point to spend some time with her during the coffee break.

"It just seems like there's so much to remember," Cindy said.

"Actually it's much easier to learn a line if you know where you'll be on stage when you're saying it," Erin told her. "Then the line and the action go together naturally."

"I sure hope so." Cindy didn't look quite convinced.

Erin gave the teenager a reassuring smile. "I'm sure of it. I wouldn't have picked you to be Cecily if I wasn't certain you could handle it."

"Thanks, Erin."

"Hey, that's what a director is for. Tell me, how's your costume coming?"

"Fine. Mrs. Powalski is a real whiz with a needle."

"She certainly is." Ellen Powalski was the director of the costume committee and therefore responsible for creating the nineteenth-century costumes required for the play's characters. Jonathan should feel right at home in his costumes, Erin decided with a grin. Both of them were suits, even if they were from a different century!

As the week's rehearsal schedule progressed Erin became more and more engrossed with the play until by the weekend she was an exhausted mass of nerves from the double load of her projects at work and the time-consuming responsibilities of being a director.

It figured that as soon as she decided to stop fighting her feelings for Jonathan, there wouldn't be time for them to get together. Although she saw him during rehearsals, there was little chance for them to be alone. Now here it was Sunday, and she had to catch up on her household chores, not because she wanted to but because she had no clean clothes and no clean dishes. She was also out of cat food, a state of affairs that Butch would not tolerate. So Erin's first priority was to go grocery shopping.

Unfortunately it felt as if half the population of Portland had also decided to show up at the local supermarket, and it took Erin an hour and a half to do thirty minutes' worth of shopping.

The phone was ringing as she let herself into her front door. While in the process of answering it, the bottom of the paper grocery bag she was holding suddenly ripped open and the oranges she'd bought dropped out and rolled all over the floor. Butch was pleased at what he perceived to be some new kind of game. Erin was not similarly amused, and it showed in her voice as she spoke into the phone.

"No, I do not want a subscription to *Golfer's Quarterly*. I told you that the last two times you called. I don't care if you are only fifteen points away from a sales trip to Hawaii," she told the persistent salesman. "I'm only one point away from a nervous breakdown!"

She'd hardly replaced the phone when it rang again. "The answer is still no!"

"What was the question?" her father asked her.

"I'm sorry, Dad. I thought you were trying to sell me *Golfer's Quarterly.*"

"Now, why would I want to do that?"

"Never mind." Erin maneuvered her feet out of her shoes and gratefully wiggled her bare toes. "How are things?"

"Things are fine," her father replied. "We had one of our busiest days ever at the cleaners yesterday."

"You really should think about hiring some extra help, especially now that Mary isn't working at the cleaners anymore. How is Mary, anyway? I haven't heard from her for a while."

"That's because you're never home long enough for her to call you."

"Is something wrong?" Erin immediately demanded. "Is the baby all right?"

"The baby's fine. Here, talk to your mother, she's the expert in the baby department."

"Hello, Erin." Her mother's voice came over the phone line. "I'm so glad we finally reached you."

"Why? What's wrong?"

"What's wrong with you that you think something has to be wrong with us before we'd call you?"

The convoluted question was typical of her mother's way of thinking. Years of experience had made Erin fluent in her mother's sometimes roundabout thought processes. Therefore she was able to translate the message: Her mother was upset because Erin hadn't made her customary bi-weekly phone call.

"I'm sorry, Mom. Things have been pretty hectic around here lately."

"You try to do too much, Erin. You always have. Are you eating properly?"

"I'm eating fine. In fact, I just went grocery shopping this morning and I now have a dozen oranges at my feet."

"That's an unusual place to keep oranges, dear. Don't you think they'd be better off in the refrigerator?"

"Probably."

Erin and her mother talked for another ten minutes as Mrs. Rossi filled Erin in on the baby's latest antics. "Have you met any nice men lately, dear?" her mother skillfully slipped in.

"I meet nice men all the time, Mother. I've told you that."

"The nicest man stopped by the cleaners the other day. He mentioned knowing you."

"Really?" Erin's reply was vague as she attempted to pick up some of the oranges before Butch rolled them under the couch.

"Yes. He's an attorney, dear, a tax attorney, and you know how stable they are."

Oh, no! "Did he happen to mention his name?"

"Yes, he did. Jonathan Garrett. It's a nice name, don't you think? He said he was working on the play with you."

I'll get him for this, Erin was silently promising herself. *Somehow, some way I'll get him for this.* Because now that her mother had met Jonathan, Erin would never hear the end of the "Isn't it time you settled down with a nice man?" routine.

Knowing her mother pumped every eligible-looking man who walked into the dry cleaners, Erin had warned Jonathan not to say anything to her parents, no matter how they might try to pump him for information. Obviously he'd ignored that warning. A knock on Erin's front door provided a welcome interruption to her mother's interrogation.

"There's someone at the door, Mom. I've got to go."

"Call us more often," her mother instructed before saying good-bye.

Erin opened her front door and found Jonathan standing on her doorstep. "You're just the person I want to talk to," she stated with ominous vehemence as she grabbed him by the arm and tugged him inside.

"Why do I get the impression that you're not trying to sweet-talk me?" Jonathan mused as he eyed her angry face.

Erin placed her clenched fists on her hips and glared at him. "You've really done it now, you know. I'll never hear the end of it."

"The end of what?" he inquired mildly, for his attention was being distracted by the sexy length of leg Erin was displaying beneath her Bermuda shorts.

"You told my mother that you were a tax attorney," she stated in an accusatory voice.

"Yes. So?"

"So? I warned you not to say anything to them, but oh, no, for once you have to shed your usual reserve and suddenly become as talkative as . . ." Erin couldn't come up with something that might be talkative, so she had to let the rest of her sentence slide.

Jonathan tore his gaze away from her legs and frowned at the mutinous expression on her face. "You mean all this upset is over a simple conversation I had with your mother?"

"Yes."

"Whew!" Mockingly he wiped a hand across his forehead in pretended relief. "For a minute there I thought it was something serious."

"You don't know my mother. This is serious."

"Do you know you have six oranges on the floor?" he asked her, having just caught sight of the citrus fruit.

"Yes, I know."

"Oh. He used the index finger of his right hand to push his glasses farther up onto the bridge of his nose. "Just checking."

Erin sighed and picked up the remaining oranges. They

were more than she could manage, so Jonathan helped her carry them, and the remainder of her groceries, to the kitchen. Luckily she hadn't made any purchases from the frozen-food department or she really would have been in trouble, for they would have melted during her extended phone conversation.

"Are you ready to leave now?" he inquired once the groceries were put away.

"Leave? Leave for where? Come to think of it, what are you doing here, anyway? I wasn't expecting you, was I?"

"No."

"Good." She folded the last paper bag and stored it in the cabinet under the kitchen sink. "For a minute there I thought my memory was going."

"Your memory's not going, but you are. With me. To the coast."

Erin's hazel eyes widened with surprise. "Whatever gave you that idea?"

"I thought of it all by myself, actually," he said with exaggerated modesty. "This is my final exam, you see. I'm proving to you how successfully you have taught me to shed my scheduled, humdrum existence and be spontaneous. So I'm spontaneously taking you to the coast for the day."

She smiled at him, appreciating the thought and regretting that she would have to turn him down.

"It's a nice idea, but I really don't have the time today."

"I'm afraid you don't understand. It's not an idea, and it's not an invitation."

"Oh? What it is then, an order?"

"No. It's about to be a *fait accompli*." Without further ado he lifted her in his arms and proceeded to head for the front door.

"Jonathan! Stop! Wait!" She wriggled wildly in his arms.

"I don't even have any shoes on!"

He detoured over to the television set, where he'd happened to spy her leather moccasins propping up the bent TV antenna. He scooped up the shoes in one hand. "Satisfied?"

"No." She grinned at him, thrilled at this unexpected romantic display. "I need my purse." He paused at the front door long enough to let her grab her large carryall purse and a lightweight waterproof jacket before he carried her outside.

"You'll have to close the door," he told her. "My hands are full."

"I can't believe you're doing this," she said, even as she obeyed his order. "And you're still not dressed casually."

"I didn't know what to wear to an abduction," he countered in a mocking voice. "I was all out of pirate's eye patches."

She gave a teasing tug to his tie. "So you wore a shirt and tie instead? Come to think of it, this vee-neck sweater looks awfully familiar too. Didn't you wear this when we were up in Mrs. Durkee's attic?"

"You're absolutely correct. How very observant of you," he said, congratulating her.

"Compared to you, I feel under-dressed."

"I like you under-dressed." Her statement was accompanied by a tickling caress behind her bare knee. "I'm sure I'd like you even better *un*dressed."

Still keeping her in his arms, Jonathan leaned over so that Erin could open the car door. He then plunked her inside, moccasins, purse, jacket, and all. In the time it took Erin to sort herself and her belongings out, Jonathan had jogged around to the driver's side of the car, slid behind the wheel, and turned on the sedan's engine.

"Put your seat belt on," he told her as he backed out of her gravel drive.

"If I have to put mine on, then you have to put yours on," she retorted as she leaned across him, intending to grab hold of the loose belt on his side of the car. Facing him, Erin extended the moment, deliberately allowing her breasts to brush against him as she reached for his seat belt.

Unable to survive the seductive temptation any longer, Jonathan slammed on the brakes. His left arm shot out to clamp her against his broad chest. "Don't move," he growled. "If you do, I could back this car right up a tree!"

"Why, Jonathan, was I bothering you?" she asked with kittenish innocence.

"Slightly."

"Only slightly?" she pouted, impudently shifting her hand up his thigh.

"Actually you're bothering me immensely, but you're welcome to check it out for yourself," he invited her, calling her bluff.

"That's all right." She wisely withdrew her hand. "I'll take your word for it."

Jonathan eased his hold on her enough for her to fasten his seat belt without any further bewitchment. As she was doing so he slipped his hand beneath the tropical print of her camp shirt and traced an invisible line around the back of her waist. In a flash Erin leaned back into her own seat and firmly fastened her own seat belt.

The drive from Portland to Oregon's northern coast was completed in just over two hours on the Sunset Highway, U.S. 26. Traffic wasn't as heavy as Erin had anticipated it would be on such a lovely day in late August. Jonathan told her that in keeping with the unscheduled ambience of the day, he had no particular destination in mind.

"We'll just go cruising," he ended up saying. "What's so funny?" he demanded as Erin laughed.

"It just sounds strange hearing someone like you using the word *cruising*."

"Can't imagine me in a low-riding Chevy with the top down, cruising up and down town looking for a chick?"

"Depends. What year was the Chevy?"

"My favorite year, nineteen fifty-five."

"Why's that your favorite year?"

"I was born in fifty-five."

Erin's mouth dropped open. "You're kidding!" She was obviously stunned. "But that would make you thirty years old."

"Right."

"I don't believe it!"

"Do you want to see my driver's license?" he inquired wryly.

"What month were you born in fifty-five?"

"In June, the eighteenth to be exact."

"I can't believe this. I'm robbing the cradle!" Erin exclaimed.

He frowned at her words. "What are you talking about?"

"You're younger than I am!"

Jonathan's ego was not assisted any by the incredulous note in her voice. "How old did you think I was?"

"Thirty-eight."

The car swerved slightly as Jonathan reacted. "Thirty-eight!"

"Yep. Does it bother you to be going out with an older woman?" she asked in a Marlene Dietrich undertone.

"How much older?"

"Six months. I was born on January twenty-nine."

"Looks like I now have another reason for choosing fifty-five as my favorite year."

Erin smiled at the backhanded compliment. She still had a

hard time placing Jonathan in her own age bracket, let alone a few months younger. Her thoughts kept her silent until they reached the city limits of Seaside. "Oh, look. There's an arts and crafts show going on in this town. Can we stop?"

"Sure."

Jonathan parked the car and they wandered through the show. Artists had their watercolors, drawings, and oils displayed on pegboards and easels while potters and sculptors showed their works on wooden shelves. Framed photographs were also widely shown as were various craft items.

Erin fell in love with a small planter made out of hand-hewn wood. The piece was meant to hang on a wall and was constructed to look like the front of a house, complete with a tiny roof. The craftsman assured Erin that the piggyback plant inside the stand was very sturdy, a good sign, since Erin did not have a green thumb. Pleased with her find, she bought it.

After strolling around the art fair they returned to the car and resumed their drive. Their next stop was at one of the numerous state parks that lined the coast. When Erin heard what Jonathan had in mind, she eyed his clothes doubtfully. "Beachcombing?"

"Something wrong with the idea?" Jonathan demanded.

She shook her head. "Not as far as I'm concerned."

"Then there's no problem."

They walked hand in hand down the narrow trail leading from the parking lot down to the wide beach. When they reached the expanse of sand, Erin kicked off her moccasins and stuffed them into her carryall. She was surprised to find Jonathan kicking off his shoes, which were moccasins similar to her own. He peeled off his dark socks, stuffed them inside the shoes, and then rolled up his slacks to just beneath his knees.

Erin couldn't help noticing that his feet were almost as nicely shaped as his hands, and that both his feet and his legs were tanned. The ocean breeze ruffled his hair, further detracting from his stuffed-shirt image.

Giving in to a whim, Erin grabbed him by the hand and yelled, "Come on!"

"Where?" He allowed himself to be tugged closer to the frothing surf.

"You have to stick your feet in the ocean."

"I do? Says who?"

"Me." Erin dashed away from him and played tag with the waves.

Jonathan cautiously dipped one toe in the water, grimaced at the cold, and retreated to dryer ground, where he watched Erin's animated game with amusement. With her hair blowing free and her shirt plastered to her very feminine body, she looked like a mermaid. Except for the legs. His eyes again slid down her long legs, from the tops of her thighs to the soles of her bare feet.

At that moment Erin turned and caught him staring at her. Her heart skipped a beat and then went into double time. Suddenly she felt unaccountably self-conscious.

As if reading her mind, Jonathan smiled at her and held out his hand. The simple gesture banished all traces of her uneasiness. She slid her hand into his and shot him a sideways grin.

Without saying a word they set off down the beach in a course parallel to the ocean. The silence between them was comfortable as they checked the sand for twisted bits of driftwood. Erin found the first piece.

She triumphantly held the driftwood aloft and demanded, "What does this look like to you?"

"A piece of driftwood."

"Besides that."

Jonathan studied the item a bit closer. "It looks a bit like my fifty-five low-riding Chevy."

"Then this piece must be for you." She handed over the newfound treasure to him.

They walked farther until Jonathan found an appropriately shaped piece of driftwood for Erin.

"It reminds me of Butch when he's all sprawled out and asleep," she said. "Thank you."

"You're welcome."

Erin lowered her voice to a seductive whisper. "Know what I want to do?"

"No, what?" Jonathan's imagination ran wild with erotic possibilities.

"Build a sand castle."

That was not one of the possibilities he'd been anticipating. Before he could recover, Erin dropped to the sandy beach and began digging.

To her surprise Jonathan dropped down beside her. "You'll ruin your slacks," she warned him.

He shrugged indifferently. "They'll dry-clean."

And so they both set to work on building the best-looking sand castle ever made. What they ended up with was a slightly lopsided fortification that bore little resemblance to a fairy-tale castle. Its off-balance appearance was a result of the three-tiered tower that Jonathan had constructed on one corner and which Erin was supposed to duplicate on the other. Somehow her tower ended up looking more like the leaning Tower of Pisa than anything else.

To her amusement and amazement Jonathan really got into the castle-making. He found a discarded paper cup and used it to form towers that matched. A flat piece of wood formed a drawbridge over the moat, and a loose feather became the royal banner. Watching him work, Erin couldn't help but wonder about this man who wore a tie while building a castle in the sand. Would she ever figure him out?

CHAPTER SEVEN

Memories of their day on the beach remained with Erin the next morning at work. But it was the memory of Jonathan's impassioned good-night kiss that was responsible for her dreamy expression—an expression that was noted by more than one coworker. Erin easily sidestepped the speculation and concentrated on completing the layout she was working on.

Her efforts were interrupted by her department head, Carl Mather. "Erin, Mr. Andrews in Marketing would like to see you right away."

Erin frowned at the news. She'd never even met Mr. Andrews, although she'd heard of him. He was the Vice-President of Marketing. "Do you know why he wants to see me?"

Carl shrugged. "His secretary didn't say. She just said you were to go directly to his office in the East Tower. Fifth floor. And bring along that last annual report you worked on."

Erin knew she was but a relatively small cog in Westcon's corporate wheel, and for the life of her she couldn't figure out why her presence was being demanded in the swank environs of the executive East Tower. The graphic arts department was located in the smaller West Tower of Westcon's corporate headquarters with what Erin mockingly referred to as the rest of the worker ants. The complex itself was roughly shaped like an hourglass with the two towers connected by a glass-enclosed walkway.

Westcon Corporation was a conglomerate with more holdings than Erin could keep track of. In the last year alone they'd acquired a nationwide chain of fast-food restaurants, a record company, a winery, and a lumber mill. She'd been working in the Graphic Arts department of the corporation for just over three years now, and in all that time this was only her second visit to the so-called Ivory Tower. Her last visit had been during her initiation tour on her first day of work.

One thing was certain: The decorating was much nicer over here, Erin decided while waiting for an elevator. Plush carpeting, expensive limited-edition prints on the walls, indoor atrium. Not bad.

When the elevator doors slid open, she stepped inside and punched the button marked "5." As she was smoothly whisked upstairs, she studied the annual report she held in her hand. It looked all right to her; in fact, it was one of her best efforts, so why was she being hauled into Marketing?

Fifteen minutes later Erin walked out of Mr. Andrews's office with a dazed smile on her face. The vice-president had been so impressed with the work she'd done in designing the layout of the annual report that he'd wanted to meet her and congratulate her personally. He'd even mentioned the possibility of a bonus.

Relieved that the news was good and not bad, Erin didn't pay much attention to the route she was taking through the mazelike office configuration until she suddenly realized that she should have reached the elevators by now. Since she hadn't, she must have taken a wrong turn somewhere. Intent on backtracking, Erin abruptly turned around and rammed into someone behind her.

"I'm sorry," she murmured. "I wasn't looking . . ." Her voice trailed away as she realized who it was she'd run into. "Jonathan! What are you doing here?"

Jonathan frowned at her. "I was just about to ask you the same thing." He hardly recognized her. She wore a navy skirt and a lilac blouse, which, while possessing more flair than most business attire, were still much more conservative than her usual outfits. "Are you here to see me?"

"No, I work here."

Jonathan looked stunned. "Here?"

"Well, not exactly here. Actually I work over there." She pointed to the West Tower, visible through the expanse of glass lining one side of the hallway. "The Graphic Arts department is over there."

"Oh, my God."

"It's not that bad," Erin murmured, eyeing the other building.

"Yes, it is. You work for Westcon?"

"Yes."

"So do I."

"Really? Small world, huh?"

"And getting smaller all the time," he muttered, half under his breath. "You do realize that Westcon has a strict policy forbidding dating among its employees, don't you?"

"Yes. So?"

"So? So we broke that rule."

Erin was about to say, "It's a dumb rule, anyway," when she was interrupted by Jonathan's angry voice.

"Why didn't you tell me you worked at Westcon?" He was glaring at her as if she'd committed a cardinal sin.

"Why didn't *you* tell me *you* worked at Westcon?" she shot back, refusing to take the blame he was so readily dishing out.

"It never occurred to me that you might work here." Jonathan shoved an impatient hand through his dark hair. "I didn't even know we had a graphic arts department."

"And it never occurred to me that you might be employed there. I thought you worked for a law firm."

Jonathan's attention was suddenly diverted from Erin to a weasely-looking character loitering in the hallway a short distance away from them. Jonathan had no trouble identifying Lewis Newton, a bootlicking attorney from the legal department who was forever keeping his eyes and ears open for information that might assist him in his advancement up the corporate ladder. Now that there was an opening in the senior ranks of the department, Jonathan was only too well aware that Lewis had his sights on it. Jonathan, however, was first in line to get the promotion, and he had no intention of providing any fodder for the other man's mud-slinging.

Erin watched Jonathan's expression switch from anger to distant disapproval.

"We'll talk later," he informed her in a brusque voice.

"Don't bother," she flared, disillusioned by his dismissal. "There's nothing left to say." Calling upon her skills as an actress, Erin withdrew herself from Jonathan and stared at him as if he were a complete stranger. "I'm sorry I ran into you." She walked by him with regal indifference.

Jonathan was about to follow her when his name was called by Lewis.

"Mr. R. wants to see you in his office. Nice-looking woman," Lewis tacked on with a knowing glance at Erin's fast-departing figure. "Does she work here?"

Jonathan didn't even bother answering the other man's question. He knew that if he said anything in that moment, it was liable to be violent.

Lewis was not discouraged by Jonathan's failure to take the bait. For the first time in months Lewis saw a way of nailing the supposedly perfect Jonathan Garrett. Lewis had overheard enough of the conversation Jonathan had had with Erin whatever-her-name-was from the Graphic Arts department to know that the lead was worth following. Where there's smoke, there's fire, and Jonathan and Erin had been billowing plenty of smoke. All Lewis had to do was catch Garrett in a compromising situation with Erin.

Of course, he'd need corroborating evidence to prove that Garrett had flagrantly violated corporate policy. A simple phone call to his contact in the personnel department should give him enough information about this woman Erin to get him started. Then he planned on keeping very close tabs on Garrett.

Unaware of the Machiavellian plans Lewis was hatching, Jonathan made his way to Mr. R.'s office. Mr. Rahmsbottom, or Mr. R. as he was called within the department, was the stern-faced, ultraconservative head of Westcon's legal department, a department that not only included tax lawyers but a team of other lawyers specializing in every aspect of corporate law. Individual divisions included contracts and mergers, Securities and Exchange regulations, as well as Jonathan's division of corporate taxes. The promotion Jonathan had been working so hard for was that of Senior Legal Counsel for his division.

Mr. R. had shown an almost avuncular interest in Jonathan's career since Jonathan had first started working for Westcon two years ago. After working in one of Westcon's satellite offices in Boston for four months, Jonathan had been transferred here to Portland at Mr. R.'s request. The older man had met Jonathan on one of his lightning tours and had been impressed by the younger man's seriousness and dependability. Ever since then Mr. R. had taken it upon himself to provide professional guidance to Jonathan, whether it was wanted or not.

"See what you can do with this tax ruling so that it can be put to our organization's benefit," Mr. R. told Jonathan.

Mr. R. preached corporate loyalty with zealous fervor, and

today was no exception. As Jonathan sat in Mr. R.'s office listening to his boss elocute on the impropriety of corporations paying taxes, Erin was steaming in her West Tower cubicle. Brightly colored burlap-covered dividers formed temporary walls dividing the office. Normally Erin would have preferred to work in one large open space where she could interact with the other three artists, but for once she appreciated the semi-privacy.

It had been a surprise discovering that Jonathan worked for Westcon, but it had been a shock to hear him dismiss her so ruthlessly. His message had been clear: His career interests were of primary importance to him. Nothing and no one would stand in his way. Since Erin was a Westcon employee, she was therefore off-limits to him. What's more, he apparently didn't even want to acknowledge knowing her.

That was fine by her. She hadn't wanted to get involved with him in the first place. As far as she was concerned, Jonathan Garrett was pond scum! She as much as told her sister such when she stopped by to visit Mary after work.

"Men stink!" Erin declared as she juggled the baby on her knee.

"Here, you'd better give my daughter to me before you bounce her dinner right back up." Mary took the baby and settled her down in the bassinet. "Don't pay any attention to your Aunt Erin," Mary advised the infant. "She's just in a snit."

"I am not in a snit," Erin protested.

"Bad choice of words," Mary agreed. "Actually it sounds more like you're on the rampage. Is there any particular reason for your mood? Are you against the entire male race or is there one in particular that you're angry with?"

"One in particular."

"What's his name?"

Erin answered without thinking. "Jonathan."

Mary's interest was piqued. "Not the same Jonathan who's a tax attorney?"

"You've been talking to Mom," Erin said accusingly.

"Guilty as charged. So go on, tell me. What did this Jonathan do to make you so angry?"

"How do I know you won't tell Mom every word I say?" Erin countered.

"Because I never told her about any of your other scrapes. Like the time when you were sixteen and you climbed into our bedroom window at two in the morning . . ."

"All right. I suppose I can trust you."

Mary grinned at her sister. "You know you can. So tell me. What's he done?"

"He works for Westcon."

"That's it?"

"The corporation has a strict no dating policy for its employees. As soon as Jonathan discovered that I work for Westcon, he treated me like I was a leper." Erin's eyes darkened with anger and disillusionment.

"Who thought up this no-dating policy? It sounds feudal to me."

"It is feudal," Erin agreed. "But then, so's Jonathan. His sole allegiance is to his corporation."

"So what are you going to do about it?" Mary demanded.

"Nothing. It's just as well that things worked out this way. Getting involved with him would have been a bad move on my part, anyway."

"What makes you say that?"

"He's in the play I'm directing. It never would have worked."

The arrival of Mary's husband precluded Erin's saying more. After greeting her brother-in-law she turned down an invitation to stay for dinner and made her departure.

Erin didn't feel like going home yet, so she stopped at a fast-food restaurant for dinner. Then she stopped at a super-market and bought a Sara Lee devil's food cake. She was in the mood to pig out tonight.

The sun was just setting as Erin pulled the Voyager into her drive. Butch eagerly greeted her as soon as she entered the gatehouse. He, too, had a fondness for chocolate cake. "Down, Butch. This cake's got my name on it."

Erin's mood wasn't improved any by going into the kitchen and finding that the dishes she'd meant to wash yes-terday were still soaking in the sink. She'd gotten back late last night after spending the day with Jonathan. Jonathan . . . Just thinking about him made her bang the dirty pots and pans with such vehemence that Butch ran for cover.

It was a good thing there wasn't a rehearsal scheduled for tonight, Erin thought to herself as she scrubbed out a frying pan. She needed more time before she'd be able to face Jona-than again without doing him bodily harm!

Feeling the need for some music, she switched on her stereo with soapy fingers and set the volume way up, glad that she had no neighbors nearby to disturb. She finished the dishes and cleaned her kitchen to the music from the Broadway production of *Cats*. She then went on to wash a load of clothing and stick it in the compact-sized dryer before she took a break.

She'd restrained herself from digging into the chocolate cake by promising herself the decadent pleasure of con-suming the dessert while lying in the midst of a fragrant bubble bath. The stereo had shut itself off once the cassette had finished. Now the sound of the gatehouse's noisy plumbing filled the air as Erin ran the water for her bath. She selected an almond bath oil from her collection and added a generous capful to the hot water.

Moments later she was immersed up to her chin in a tub full of bubbles. Reaching over, she grabbed the metal package containing her dessert and leaned back against the antique porcelain tub with a fork in hand. She'd eaten her way through three-quarters of the cake before the water turned cool and the bubbles burst. Sighing regretfully, she set the food aside, pulled the plug, and climbed out of the tub.

She'd just toweled herself dry and slipped on her favorite nightgown when she heard someone pounding on her front door. Pulling on the matching robe to the indigo peignoir set, she cautiously made her way to the living room. "Who is it?" she called out.

"It's Jonathan." His voice reached her clearly through the wooden door. "Let me in."

"Forget it!"

"Erin, we have to talk."

"No, we don't."

"Erin, I'm not going away. I'm going to stay out here until you let me in."

"You can stay out there all night for all I care!"

His continued assault on her door coincided with the ringing of her telephone. Erin chose to answer the phone rather than the door. "Hello?"

"Erin, it's your mother." Mrs. Rossi paused a moment as she heard the racket in the background. "What on earth is going on over there?"

"Nothing, Mother."

"Who's making all that noise?"

"Uh, Butch."

"Since when has Butch learned how to talk?" Mrs. Rossi demanded as she heard a decidedly male voice raised in anger.

"It's nothing to get upset about," Erin hastily assured her mother.

"I am upset. It sounds like you're under attack! Should I call the police?"

The idea of having Jonathan arrested for disorderly conduct was tempting, but Erin resisted. "I can handle things here, Mother. There's no need to call the police."

It took Erin several minutes to convince her mother not to call the authorities. Luckily Jonathan had either gone away or decided to be quiet, because the pounding and shouting had stopped.

"Now, you're sure you'll be all right?" Mrs. Rossi demanded one last time.

"I'll be fine, Mother." The remainder of her reassurance was muffled by a male hand that had appeared out of nowhere to clamp itself across her mouth. Erin was about to practice her limited knowledge of self-defense on her assailant when she realized that it was Jonathan!

He took the phone from Erin's stunned fingers. "This is Jonathan Garrett, Mrs. Rossi. You can safely leave your daughter in my hands. Fine. No problem. I'll have her call you later. Good night." He hung up the phone, still keeping Erin effectively muzzled with his right hand.

Her anger grew out of bounds, and she bit the hand that covered her mouth, effectively nipping the sensitive palm of his hand. "Ouch! Dammit, calm down!" Jonathan growled. He pulled her back against his chest, his arms managing her until the worst of her anger had passed. "Are you ready to be reasonable now?"

She nodded. Reasonable was in the eye of the beholder.

The moment he set her free, she took two giant steps away from him and turned to face him, ready to do battle. What she wasn't ready for was his appearance!

He looked nothing like the Jonathan she was accustomed to seeing. He wasn't wearing a suit. A pair of well-washed jeans molded his long legs while a black T-shirt clung to his broad shoulders. Even more importantly, he wasn't wearing his glasses. His blue eyes glared at her.

Erin was stunned by the transformation. Clark Kent had just turned into Superman! Jonathan was more than merely good-looking, he was gorgeous. He was also furious. He was not, however, a stuffed shirt, and in that instant Erin suddenly realized that he never had been.

CHAPTER EIGHT

"Of all the low-down, conniving, sneaking, rotten tricks!" Erin was so angry, she was shaking. The blinders had finally been removed and she saw everything with abrupt clarity. "You never needed any lessons in *joie de vivre,* did you? You never were a stuffed shirt! This was all one big joke for you, wasn't it?"

Jonathan's voice was harsh as he said, "Does it look like I'm laughing?"

Erin refrained from commenting on how he looked as another thought came to mind. "How did you get in here?"

"Your bedroom window was open. I climbed in."

His curt announcement confirmed what Erin had already suspected. The change in Jonathan was not only superficial; it went beyond a simple pair of jeans and a T-shirt. The casual attire and the ease with which he wore it merely substantiated the fact that this Jonathan Garrett was a man to be reckoned with. His civilized veneer had vanished. She now realized that it was merely a mask he used to disguise the true forcefulness of his personality. Now that the mask was gone, he looked perfectly capable of dangerous undertakings such as breaking and entering.

Erin saw red. "Did you make a special trip all the way out here just to rub my nose in the mistake I made? Is that why you decided to drop the pretense?"

"You're always jumping to conclusions, most of them inaccurate. That's how this misunderstanding got started. From the moment you first laid eyes on me you were so certain that I was a stuffed shirt, I couldn't resist playing along."

"I saw what you wanted me to see," Erin retorted. "If you'd looked like this the first time we'd met, I would never have labeled you a stuffed shirt."

"That's exactly the point I wanted to make. You judged me by my appearance. So does Westcon. I learned the hard way that I don't fit the image of a serious corporate tax attorney, and if I wanted to be taken seriously in my professional life, then I had to look the part. You do the same thing, to a lesser degree. When I saw you today in the hallway at Westcon, I almost didn't recognize you. I'd never seen you dressed so conservatively."

"I'll grant you that we all assume a certain image at work, but that doesn't explain why you kept up the pretense after work. Do you even wear glasses, or were they just part of your disguise?" she demanded with angry sarcasm.

"The glasses are real, I'm wearing contacts now. And I kept up the pretense, as you call it, because I wanted to get to know you better."

"So you decided to lie to me?"

He took exception to her accusation. "I may have misled you, but I never lied to you."

"From where I'm standing there isn't much difference between the two. And you still haven't answered my original question. Why drop the pretense now?"

"I never intended to hang on to the stuffed-shirt image as long as I did, but you seemed to be responding to it so well—" Jonathan broke off his explanation as he immediately realized that that might not be the most diplomatic way of putting it.

He was too late. Erin's burning anger flared into the sizzling danger zone and she lashed out. "Why tamper with success, right? So you did whatever it took to try to con me into going to bed with you. It must have been quite a shock to find out you've wasted all this time and effort on someone who's taboo to you."

"What are you talking about?" Jonathan demanded with curt impatience. "Taboo?"

"I'm talking about your beloved corporation's golden rule: Thou shall not covet thy coworker's body. But then, you're already well versed with the rule, aren't you? You're the one who reminded me about it when we met in the hallway this morning. Is that why you came here tonight and broke into my home? To warn me to keep quiet about having spent time with you?"

"No, that is not why I came here tonight." Anger lent his words a gritty texture. "I broke in because you childishly refused to open your door or answer the phone when I called you earlier. I came to try to explain things, maybe work something out."

"See if you couldn't have your cake and eat it too?" Erin suggested bitterly.

For one brief moment Jonathan thought he saw pain lurking behind the anger flashing in Erin's eyes. The glimpse was enough to prompt him to make one last attempt at an explanation. "Look, this isn't all my fault. If you'd told me you worked at Westcon, we could have anticipated this problem."

But Erin had already retreated once again behind her temper. "*You* could have told me *you* worked at Westcon just as easily."

"So it's a stalemate, is it?"

"You got it. Which means no more uninvited visits. From now on we'll see each other only at rehearsals."

"If that's the way you want it, fine." His expression became remote.

Erin then made the tactical error of sarcastically stating, "How kind of you to give me your approval." She'd been so caught up in their fight that she'd forgotten how vulnerable she was, standing there in her nightgown. The silky robe she wore over it had been designed more for decoration than modesty, and it displayed a generous amount of cleavage. That fact was brought home to her now as Jonathan's blue eyes darkened with passion, lending his face an ominously dangerous expression.

Erin took an instinctive step backward, but it was too late. His hands shot out and clamped themselves around her arms, halting her in her tracks. An instant later he'd pulled her toward him with such force that Erin almost had the air knocked out of her.

Through the thin silk of her apparel she could feel the taut muscles of his arm as he braced it at an angle across her back, from her left shoulder clear down to her right hip. The move effectively pinned her to him. His other hand was now free to cup the back of her head, his fingers surging into the darkness of her hair.

"Brave words," he growled, "but let's see you try to mock this. . . ."

Her exclamation of outrage was silenced before it even began as his mouth captured hers. She tried to arch away from him, but that only served to bring her more fully against him. He was aroused, taut and straining beneath the thin denim of his jeans. Realizing that she was only worsening the situation, she stopped struggling.

She expected his kiss to be an assault, but she was mistaken. There was no angry brutality. Instead he took her lips with a possessive fierceness. His mouth engulfed hers, moving over her lips and parting them as if satisfying a burning need.

Erin's objections were submerged by a fiery onslaught of sensations. She felt the thrust of his tongue followed by the thrust of his hips, a bold combination that was intensely erotic. The delicate silk of her robe swirled around his legs. With a raspy groan Jonathan hauled her even closer. Their contact was becoming increasingly intimate when the shrill demands of the telephone shattered the moment.

Erin resumed her struggles. Like a steel trap sprung open, Jonathan abruptly released her from his restrictive hold. Backing away from him, she paused at a safe distance to regain her breath, her anger, and her bearings. The moment she'd gathered all three, she intrepidly marched over to her front door, unlocked it, and jerked it open. She fixed a menacing glare on Jonathan. "You'd better leave. Right now!"

Jonathan reacted by hurtling a challenge at her. "How long do you think you can deny what's between us?"

"Until hell freezes over!"

"Fine." He reached the door in three long strides. For a moment Erin was afraid he might take her in his arms again, but he stormed right past her. "We'll see how strictly professional you can be."

"Yes, we will. Starting right now. Good-bye, Mr. Garrett!" she shouted with icy formality before slamming the door and bolting it.

Only then was Erin able to answer the telephone. "Hello? Yes, I'm fine, Mother. What was Jonathan doing here?" Erin grimly noted the sound of gravel spinning beneath the tires of Jonathan's car as he accelerated out of her driveway. "He was displaying his acting abilities, Mother, that's all."

Erin did not sleep well that night. She tried drinking herbal tea, reading, counting sheep. Nothing worked. She was up and dressed before it was even light outside.

As she studied her appearance in the mirror Jonathan's words about a corporate image unintentionally came to mind. So she didn't wear her Bermuda shorts or her pink-

and-black bowling shirt to work. What did that prove? She'd never pretended to be something she wasn't. Jonathan had.

Erin turned away from the mirror. So far her anger at Jonathan had insulated her from the pain of his deception. But that form of anesthetic was beginning to wear off, and when it did, she knew that coping wouldn't be easy.

In light of her almost sleepless night it wasn't surprising that Erin was drained by noon. In an attempt to rejuvenate herself she left the Westcon complex during her lunch hour and drove to a nearby restaurant. Had she looked in her rearview mirror, she might have noticed the white car following her.

Lewis had been trailing Erin ever since his contact in the personnel department had given him her full name and address yesterday. He'd followed her home last night, after having made an earlier stop at a camera store where he bought a powerful telephoto lens for the expensive camera he owned but rarely used. He'd hung around her place awhile last night, not really expecting to see anything worth recording his first time out.

To his surprise Jonathan did show up. Unfortunately Lewis hadn't yet had the chance to perfect his use of the telephoto lens, and the pictures that he'd taken and rushed to a one-hour film developing lab this morning were blurred and unusable. So Lewis had resumed his surveillance, anonymously calling the Graphic Arts department and garnering the information that Erin's lunch hour was scheduled at one o'clock.

Although Lewis followed her to the restaurant and kept tabs on her during the entire hour, he did not see any sign of Jonathan. Frustrated, Lewis returned to the office and put the second half of his plan into action.

Lewis began his smear campaign against Jonathan with an offhand comment to Mr. R., couched amid concern for a fellow attorney. "They are strictly rumors, so far, sir." Lewis spoke with careful deference. "I'd just hate to see Jonathan get into any trouble as a result of it. I know he's up for that promotion, and I wouldn't want anything to reflect badly on us here in Legal."

"Wise move, Newton," Mr. R. congratulated the younger man. "It's always best to deal with these things before they become a problem. I appreciate your bringing it to my attention."

"I'm relieved you see it that way, sir. I wouldn't want you to think I was carrying tales."

"Nonsense. I know exactly what motivated you, my boy." Mr. Rahmsbottom hadn't risen to his position without being able to read men's motivations. He was well aware that Lewis Newton's career plans were in conflict with Jonathan's. But if there were even a hint of truth to the gossip about Jonathan, then he intended to nip the problem in the bud by having a heart-to-heart with Jonathan—as soon as possible.

A little while later Jonathan walked into his office.

"Sit down, Jonathan."

Jonathan did so, feeling unusually impatient with this interruption. The case he was working on demanded a great deal of legal research. Jonathan had been in the midst of sifting through the accrued legal citations that a paralegal assistant had gathered for him when he received the call from Mr. R's secretary, Mrs. Bunt.

Jonathan had a sudden inkling that Erin might be the topic of this unscheduled discussion. But then, she'd been in his thoughts all day, so he couldn't say if his suspicions were based on tangible evidence or were a result of her habitual presence in his mind.

Mr. R. decided to get right to the point. "I called you into my office because I've heard some alarming gossip regarding you and a female employee here at Westcon." Mr. R. studied Jonathan's expression, but all he discerned was a brief flash of anger, not guilt. "Now, I'm sure these statements are no doubt exaggerated, but I thought it best to stave off any future difficulties by reviewing the corporation's policies in such matters—and the reasoning behind these policies. As you are aware, Westcon does have a strict ruling against dating or any other type of romantic entanglements between its employees. This is true at all levels of the corporate structure, from the mail room right up to the presidential suite. The reason for such a policy is simple. Business and pleasure never mix. Personal problems are invariably brought into the office. The next thing you know, accusations of favoritism will start pouring in. The possibility of sexual harassment on the job is also increased by inter-employee dating. Surely you can see the problems that could arise from such a situation?"

Jonathan nodded grimly.

"Good. Then there's nothing more to discuss. With your promotion almost in the bag we don't want to do anything to rock the boat right now."

Under other circumstances Jonathan might have been tempted to smile at Mr. R.'s overuse of metaphors. But at the moment all he could think of was slugging Lewis Newton, for Jonathan had no doubt that Lewis was the source of the "alarming gossip." While a physical confrontation with Newton might be momentarily rewarding, it would not help Jonathan in his quest for this promotion. So, for the time being, all he could do was play it cool.

Unfortunately, playing it cool was becoming increasingly difficult to do, especially when it concerned Erin. Jonathan purposely attended that night's rehearsal session without benefit of a three-piece suit or his glasses. While his attire wasn't as casual as the jeans and T-shirt he'd worn while climbing through Erin's bedroom window last night, his tan slacks and red shirt were more than sufficient to cause a stir.

"Jonathan, is that you?" Martha exclaimed. Her astonishment came complete with a classic double take. "I barely recognized you! My dear boy, you're a hunk! If only I were ten years younger and you ten years older . . ."

From her position up in the sound-and-light booth Erin was able to hear the joshing comments and suggestions being put to Jonathan. She was also able to see the look of animated interest that each woman wore as they gazed at Jonathan with obvious delight. Did they have to be so obvious? So, he was good-looking. There was no need to drool over the man!

Determined to ignore the fawning that was going on, Erin completed her conference with Ned. They'd already gone over the lighting and sound requirements for this act, and Erin was just making some minor adjustments The sound-and-light control booth was an addition to the original building, if a four-by-six-foot space could be called an addition. Actually the boxed-in enclosure had simply been cantilevered out from the back wall and was reached by a ladder that leaned against the outside wall of the building.

Erin climbed down the ladder with surefooted precision. The canvas shoes she wore had soles thick enough that the ladder rungs didn't dig into the bottom of her feet. Upon reaching the ground, she smoothed her hands against the pleated front of her hot pink cotton slacks and then tugged up the sleeves of her boldly patterned sweatshirt, as if preparing herself for battle.

Ned remained behind in the sound-and-light booth, out of the way of trouble. He recognized the signs of Erin's temper. She might have been quiet for the time being, but it was only the calm before the storm.

Erin marched back inside the theater and made a curt

announcement. "We'll begin the final runthrough of Act Two in five minutes."

While the actors took their places Erin took note of the changes that had occurred since their last rehearsal on Saturday. The scenery committee was in the final stages of constructing the scenery for each of the play's three acts. Cans of paint, electric saws, and two-by-fours were gathered in one corner of the theater. The construction was done on those evenings when a rehearsal was not scheduled because there simply wasn't room for everything to be done at once.

Dan approached Erin with a status report on the rest of the play's production. "The set is coming along nicely, don't you think?"

Erin nodded. Act Two took place in a garden, and an old-fashioned wicker table, four chairs, and a couch had been carefully set into place.

"I've checked with the florist and they'll have someone come over during the week of final rehearsals and set up all the flowers and stuff. Let's see . . . what else . . ." Dan consulted his clipboard. "The costumes are coming along on schedule, no problem anticipated there. The printer will have the posters ready sometime next week, and I've already given the newspapers the dates of our run."

"Fine." Erin's reply was a little absentminded. Her attention was focused on Jonathan and Cindy. The teenager was blatantly flirting with him.

Erin told herself she didn't care. She told herself that the funny ache near her heart was a result of skipping dinner. And then she told herself that she'd never been a good liar. Okay, so it was jealousy. She still had a play to direct, and she had no intention of allowing Jonathan to distract her from her responsibilities.

Having silently delivered the self-help pep talk, Erin

turned her back on the goings-on between Jonathan and Cindy to ask Dan, "Does the florist understand that we need an English garden and not a tropical jungle?"

"Yes. They promised us some blooming rosebushes, among other things. Don't worry about it. They've been donating their services for three years now and haven't goofed up yet."

In exchange for providing the flowers and greenery whenever a set needed it, the florist received a special acknowledgment in the program. Which reminded Erin . . . "What about the program covers?"

"The proofs won't be done until after Labor Day. I'll show them to you as soon as I get them so you can decide which one you want to go with."

"Okay." Erin checked her watch. "We're about to begin." She joined Wanda at their worktable, located in the middle of where the audience's front row would be when the chairs were set up. Dan chose to watch the performance from the far corner of the room.

"Places," Wanda requested.

The actors hastened to their assigned places, and the rehearsal began.

It went well. Erin was glad something finally was.

"That was very good, everyone," Erin congratulated them at the end of the second act. "Keep up that energy level and we'll be a hit. That's it for tonight. See you all tomorrow night at eight."

Everyone trudged on downstairs to the dressing room where they'd left their personal belongings, but Erin stayed at her worktable. She made a few notes in the prompt book and studied the marks that Wanda had made in those places where someone had either forgotten a line or spoken it incorrectly.

She thought everyone had left to go over to the Lion's Inn

Pub when Jonathan's voice reached her from the semidarkness backstage. "I want to talk to you."

"As long as it's about the play. Your acting ability is remarkable, you know." Her tone of voice robbed the words of their complimentary nature. "But then, you and the character you're portraying in this play have a lot in common. No doubt you feel an affinity with John Worthing."

Jonathan took a few leisurely steps toward her. "What makes you say that?"

"Come now," she drawled in a mocking voice, "surely you've already noticed the similarities? John Worthing was one person in the country and quite another when he visited the city. In the country he was the sedate Mr. Worthing, while in London he was the dashing Ernest. Not unlike your own little charade."

"If you're done drawing literary analogies, I've got an important matter to discuss with you. Apparently the rumors have already started floating around Westcon that you and I have been seeing each other."

"Afraid you're going to lose your job?" she taunted him.

"No, afraid *you* might lose *yours*. I don't want to be responsible for your getting into trouble."

The word *responsible* grated on her already exposed nerves, spurring her into attacking. "How noble of you. But I can take care of myself. So don't waste your time worrying about me. Spend it memorizing your lines for Act Three, because I will not allow anything or anyone to foul up this play!"

Anger tautened the planes of his face and chilled the midnight-blue of his eyes. "The show must go on, is that it?"

"That's it," she said, confirming it with a curt nod.

"Fine."

"Great."

Only it wasn't, and they both knew it.

CHAPTER NINE

"How long is this silent war between you and Jonathan going to continue?" Dan asked Erin three days later. "Whenever you two are together, the air is thick enough to cut with a knife."

"It's not—us, it's nervous anxiety that's thickening the air," Erin replied as she gathered up her notes. She and Dan were the last ones left in the theater. "You know, stage fright—the jitters."

"Come on, you can't con me, Erin. I may not have been a member of the Village Players as long as you have, but I've been around enough to distinguish between jitters and antagonism."

"When have I been antagonistic?" Erin demanded.

Dan was getting impatient with Erin's refusal to acknowledge what was going on between her and Jonathan. "Do you want me to list each occasion?"

Her hazel eyes flashed with imminent anger. "You've made a list?"

Dan held out his hands in a conciliatory gesture. "Look, I'm not trying to butt into your private business, but whatever went on between you and Jonathan is beginning to affect the rest of us. And that kind of tension is hazardous while rehearsing a play. We've got enough tension of our own."

Erin sagged in defeat. "I don't want anything interfering with the success of this play."

"I know you don't. Isn't there some way you and Jonathan can settle your differences?"

"Kiss and make up, you mean?" she asked with bitter

humor. "I'm afraid not. Jonathan kisses me and he kisses his job good-bye."

Dan frowned in confusion. "What's that supposed to mean?"

"It means that we both work for the same company, Westcon."

"Yeah, is that a problem?"

"Yeah, when said company has a strict no-dating policy for its employees." Erin made a concerted effort to lighten the conversation. "You know, maybe you should take partial blame for this mess." Her words were half serious, half teasing.

"Me? Why? What did I do?"

"You were the one who brought Jonathan into the Village Players."

"So? He's a natural actor."

"You can say that again," Erin muttered, thinking how well he'd played his own deception.

"How was I to know that it would matter that you work for the same company? So what are you going to do about it?"

"Why does everyone keep asking me that question?" Erin muttered impatiently, remembering how her sister had asked her the same thing.

"Probably because you're a mover and a shaker. If you don't like something, you make an effort to change things."

"Some things can't be changed."

"Well, the overwhelming antagonism between you and Jonathan is going to have to change," Dan stated with candid bluntness.

Erin stiffened at the unintended criticism. "I didn't realize it was that obvious."

"To outsiders it might not be. But we've become a pretty tight-knit group in the three and a half weeks we've been rehearsing. We've almost reached the halfway point, you know," Dan added almost parenthetically.

"I know." Opening night was exactly four weeks away.

"Then you also know that things will be getting even more harried from here on out."

"You're right, as usual." Erin rubbed a weary hand across the aching muscles at the back of her neck. "I'll work harder at keeping my personal feelings to myself."

It wasn't easy. Erin had to train herself to see Jonathan only as the character he was playing in the Oscar Wilde play and not as either the man who'd kissed her with such passion up in Mrs. Durkee's attic or the renegade who'd climbed in through her bedroom window. On one level she was successful. Her deliberately even-tempered attitude lessened the degree of overall tension at the theater. But Erin knew her performance wasn't fooling Jonathan.

The arrival of Labor Day a few days later marked the transition from August to September. As they did every Labor Day, the Rossi family gathered at Kelley Point Park for their annual barbecue. The large park had been created on the marshlands where the Willamette River joined the mighty Columbia River in the northwestern tip of Portland.

The place had long been a favorite of Erin's. She loved watching the river traffic. It reminded her that Portland was not only the City of Roses but also an international port with excellent access to the Pacific Ocean provided by the Willamette River. Erin had always had a special fascination for the sturdy tugboats as they maneuvered freighters, pushed loaded barges, or towed log rafts along the busy waterway.

"I thought I'd find you down here," her sister Mary commented as she joined Erin. "Come on, the food's ready. Wait till you taste what Dad's done to his special barbecue sauce this year!"

Every Labor Day Joe Rossi concocted his secret recipe, adding new ingredients each time so that no two batches ever tasted the same. Usually Erin was the first in line with her plate in hand, ready to take the barbecued chicken off the grill. But Erin hadn't been her usual cheerful self today, and Mary had a sneaking suspicion that she knew why—Jonathan Garrett.

Obviously Erin did not want to discuss Jonathan. She'd even gone so far as to deliberately change the subject when their matchmaking mother had brought the man's name up earlier in the day. Mary honored Erin's desire for privacy and didn't press her sister for details. Instead Mary tried to cheer Erin up with recollections of their childhood.

"Do you remember how much you used to want to be a tugboat captain?" Mary asked.

The ploy was successful. Erin's face lost its brooding melancholy, and a reluctant grin made its way across her lips. "Sure I do."

"You were what, a sophomore in high school?"

Erin nodded. "Mom was shocked when I told her I wanted to join the Merchant Marines instead of going to college."

The story led to others about their teenage years as Erin and Mary walked back to the barbecue site. Mary's husband Bill was tickling baby Kathleen as she lay on his lap. Their mother was dishing out generous helpings of coleslaw and pasta salad while their father stood guard over the grill, wearing his official apron and brandishing a pair of metal tongs.

"There you two are," Joe Rossi exclaimed. "Finally! I thought you'd fallen in."

"I was just preventing Erin from signing on as a tugboat

captain," Mary retorted.

"Maybe Kathleen will want to be a tugboat captain when she grows up," Erin mused with a fond glance at the baby.

"She's going to be the first lady president," Bill declared with paternal pride. "See this chin? It's very determined. And she's already displaying leadership qualities."

"If you're talking about the way she tried to make a grab for Butch's tail at my house, I'm afraid that doesn't qualify," Erin retorted as she took a paper plate from her mother.

"Today a cat, tomorrow the world!" Bill prophesied.

For a while Erin was able to forget her problems as she teased and laughed with her family. The chicken was delicious, although Erin didn't eat as much as usual. But after the food had been consumed, the grill doused, and the fixings put away, Erin bowed out of the three-way game of Frisbee between Bill, Mary, and her father.

"I'm going to go back down to the river for a bit," she told them before adding the teasing rejoinder, "No cheating while I'm gone."

Erin had some thinking to do, and she always did her clearest thinking by the river. Here she had the peace of mind to take her emotions out of the locked drawer she'd stuffed them into and examine each one. Why had she been so angry with Jonathan? Why had his deception bothered her so much? As an actress herself, she knew better than most people that everyone was playing a role to a certain extent.

Looking back on it, perhaps Jonathan had been right to say that she'd prejudged him at their very first meeting. He wasn't a stuffed shirt, yet he wasn't a devil-may-care playboy, either—despite his great looks. Ever since he'd quit wearing his corporate image to rehearsals, Jonathan had been inundated with attention from every feminine member of the cast and production crew. Even the costume mistress had taken her time over the final fitting for Jonathan's costumes, checking his measurements with unnecessary precision.

Erin had been consumed with jealousy, but actually Jonathan had given her little cause to feel that way. He'd parried the feminine attention with good humor and a grain of salt. Not the wolfish behavior of a playboy.

Perhaps that was part of the problem. Jonathan couldn't be pinned down as one type or another. He was a complex diversity of many different types. No doubt that was why he'd caught her attention and held it.

Erin's candid look at her own emotions dissolved the tight ball of anger that had been lodged within her ever since she'd discovered Jonathan's deception. Even though she'd reached no clear decision about things, at least the resentment was gone. Feeling pounds lighter, Erin rejoined her family for their game of Frisbee and wore them all out with her energetic throws.

Erin's renewed zest for living carried her right on through that week and most of the next. Her attitude frustrated Jonathan, whose desire for Erin had increased rather than diminished. He watched her constantly, he wanted her constantly. And he knew that despite Westcon's policies, he was going to have her. He had to.

Erin's run of good luck came to an abrupt screech the following Friday afternoon at work when she received a phone call from Mr. Sinaldi, the antique dealer who'd put her brass bed on layaway.

"Bad news, I'm afraid, Ms. Rossi," the man told her after identifying himself.

Erin's heart sank. "About my bed?"

" 'Fraid so."

"What happened?"

"You remember I told you that I store all my layaways in a

warehouse because I don't have enough room here in the store?"

"No, I don't remember you telling me that." Erin had thought that her bed was safely sitting where she'd seen it last month.

"Well, there was a problem at the warehouse. A fire apparently."

"My bed?"

"I don't know yet if your bed was damaged or not. The fire department has the fire out, but they haven't allowed us to go in yet. As soon as I hear anything definite, I'll let you know."

Erin was crushed. That bed was meant for her. She'd known it from the moment she'd first seen it in the window of the antique furniture store; her grandmother's hand-tatted lace bedspread would look perfect on it.

You should have charged it and taken it home with you then, she silently berated herself after hanging up the phone. But she'd taken the more sensible approach of using the store's layaway plan and made weekly installment payments. She'd only had two more payments to make and the bed would have been hers. "So much for being sensible!" she muttered in disgust.

Erin managed to put a brave front on her sagging spirits that evening at the rehearsals. Thankfully Wanda was always at her side, providing moral support. Rehearsals were now done in costume, because Erin strongly felt that everyone needed to feel as comfortable with their costume as their characters would be. That meant that all the actresses wore their long dresses while the two leading men wore the suits popular in the 1890s. The set was completed and the stage crew had already begun timing the set changes in between acts. On an average they had twelve minutes to complete the changes. Opening night was only fourteen days away.

There were no phones at the theater, so Erin couldn't call the antique dealer and demand an update. Surely by now he'd know whether or not her bed had been damaged. After all, she'd only purchased the headboard and footboard, not the mattress and springs. At what temperature did brass melt, anyway?

Jonathan noticed Erin's preoccupation immediately He wasn't feeling all that fresh himself. That's what came of nights of restless sleep and erotic dreams of making love to Erin. She'd ruined him for other women; he had no interest in satiating his desire elsewhere.

Erin was cool toward him, obeying the rules they'd set down in a moment of anger. He needled her, but she was restrained in her replies, no longer flying off the handle as she had before. Frustrated, Jonathan started looking for another way to approach her.

But so much of his free time was tied up with rehearsals for the play, as was Erin's time, that it was the day before the final technical run-through, two days before dress rehearsals and less than a week before opening night when Jonathan finally got his opportunity. It was prefixed by a phone call from Dan.

"Listen, buddy, I hate to call you so early on the one Saturday we don't have a rehearsal, but I need a favor," Dan croaked.

"What's wrong?" Jonathan asked while groggily peering at his alarm clock. "You sound terrible."

"It's the flu. I'll live, but I'm not going to be able to make it to Erin's place. I've got the final proofs of the program covers that she's got to approve today. I tried calling her but there's no answer. Do you think you could drop them off at her house for me? If she's not there, you can just leave them in her mailbox."

"No problem," Jonathan hastily assured Dan. Here was

his chance to see Erin alone while having a perfectly valid excuse for doing so.

While Jonathan was on his way to Dan's apartment to pick up the proofs, Erin was standing in her driveway, looking in dismay at her just-delivered brass bed.

"All it needs is a little polish," one of the deliverymen assured her. "We've brought along a couple cans of brass cleaner for you, no charge. And Mr. Sinaldi said to forget the last two payments you owe. He's marked your bill as paid, see?" The man handed over a bill of sale. "Where do you want us to put it?"

"In the living room, I guess. But wait, let me put down some newspapers first." Erin arranged the papers across her living room floor and placed a dropcloth across the thick pine table that served as a sideboard. The foot- and headboards were then leaned against the table before the deliverymen made their hurried departure.

Erin sank to her knees and gazed at the tarnished expanse of solid brass. The sooty pieces bore little resemblance to the gleaming bed she'd purchased. Butch was undertaking his own sniffing inspection of this new addition to his living space.

"What do you think, Butch? Is there any hope for it?"

Butch blinked at her and then nodded his head. It wasn't the first time that the cat had answered a question when she'd asked him one. By now Erin took the trait for granted.

While changing into a pair of old worn jeans and a men's denim work shirt, Erin couldn't help remembering the fantasies she'd woven around that bed.

Jonathan had played a major part in those fantasies, spurning his three-piece suits to come to her in all his masculine glory. Now those fantasies were as tarnished as the bed itself.

But Erin's pessimism didn't last long. She read the instructions on the brass polishing can carefully. After opening all the gatehouse windows to ensure proper ventilation, Erin got to work. Her mood got another boost when she saw that the cleaner did actually remove the tarnish. The bed of her dreams was still under there after all!

At that moment the man of her dreams was standing on her doorstep, preparing to lift the brass door knocker. Erin was humming under her breath as she stepped over the pile of rags and other cleaning accoutrements to answer the door. Both her humming and her breathing were temporarily suspended as soon as she opened her front door and saw Jonathan.

He was wearing a casual short-sleeved shirt and jeans, and he looked incredibly sexy. Even though she'd seen him only last night at rehearsals, somehow he looked even more magnetic standing on her front step than he did standing on the Little Theatre's thrust stage. She stared at him, her eyes revealing more than she realized.

She wanted him. Right there and then. The abruptness of her emotions stunned her almost as much as the forcefulness of them did.

Jonathan regarded her with equal desire. His eyes roved over her—from the top of her head with her haphazardly pinned-up hair, clear down to the delicately painted toenails of her bare feet. The slide of his eyes down her body was like the caressing brush of fingertips.

"What do you want?" The words left her lips in a breathy exhalation of air that hung between them, loaded with evocative meaning.

I want you. His answer was apparent by the way he was looking at her; by his absorption with the shape of her mouth, the shape of her body.

When he spoke, his polite words were at odds with his expression of raw passion. "May I come in?"

Erin glanced over her shoulder at the mess that was her living room. "Uh . . ."

Jonathan nudged her aside before she'd even realized what his intentions were. Now that he was inside she still wasn't sure of his intentions. He viewed the brass bed frame with raised eyebrows, but he made no comment. Instead he indicated a manila envelope that he held in his hand. "Dan wanted you to see these as soon as possible. The printer needs to know your decision this morning."

Printer? Decision? Erin shook off the trancelike state his arrival had put her in and took the envelope from him.

Jonathan deliberately held the package in such a way that Erin's hand was bound to brush against his. The touch was brief, but it was exhilarating to both of them. The thrill hadn't gone. Their bodies already knew what their minds had yet to comprehend.

Erin grasped for sanity. "Dan? Why didn't he come?"

"He's got the flu."

"Oh." Erin was so rattled that she forgot even to offer her regrets at the news of Dan's illness. Hoping to lessen his charismatic influence on her, Erin moved away from Jonathan. She curled up on the window seat next to Butch and pulled the proofs from their envelope. Her selection didn't take long; she chose the version with the streamlined artwork and eye-catching lettering.

When she looked up, she realized that Jonathan had picked up a rag and was calmly working on polishing the footboard. Erin called the printer and told him her selection. Since he had the original artwork there, it was no problem for him to go directly to print. The programs would be ready Monday morning. That job taken care of, Erin hung up the phone and turned to face Jonathan.

"You don't have to help me," she felt obligated to tell him.

"Four hands are better than two," he replied without breaking his polishing rhythm.

Erin couldn't argue with his logic. With both of them working the polishing job would take only one day instead of two or three. So she picked up her own rag and resumed work on the headboard.

But his analogy of hands had instigated some steamy imagery in her own mind. His hands—she'd always admired them. And she'd often wondered what kind of magic they might create on a woman's body, on *her* body. She remembered very clearly how they'd felt as they glided across her breasts. It had been heaven.

Erin's eyes were dark with erotic memories as she slid him a sidelong look. Jonathan was concentrating on his work and appeared unaware of her bemused concentration on the buffing movement of his hands.

She imagined him caressing her with equal precision. His fingers would handle her with sensual skill—rubbing back and forth, again and again. Her breasts tightened in response to her heated thoughts and desire uncurled deep within her, heavy and soft.

Her dazed eyes were glued to his hands, mesmerized by the spell. She imagined him touching her more intimately, tending to the spot that was now aching with primitive pulses of passion. Her eyes closed and her color rose. He would cup her with the palm of his hand and buff her, polishing her until she gleamed with sensual moistness.

And then he'd probe her inner secrets—melting her, absorbing her essence, acquainting himself with every nuance of her body. He'd find her weak spots. He'd cultivate them, nurturing them until she was rocking with oscillating pleasure.

"Something wrong?"

Erin opened eyes glazed with passion and stared at Jonathan's innocently impassive face. "Whhaaat?" she whispered huskily.

"Is something wrong?"

"No." She shook her head, intent on clearing the erotic images from her mind. "No." Her voice was stronger this time. "Uh, would you like a drink? Some iced tea?"

"Okay." He watched her as she walked from the room. Anticipation worked its way down his body, making him painfully aware of how much he wanted Erin. And she wanted him. He'd seen it in her eyes when he'd first knocked on her door, and there was no mistaking it in her face as she'd stood beside him a moment ago. Jonathan nodded as a devilish smile lit his face. She'd wanted him all right, and by the end of the day she was going to have him!

They both knew it. Even as Erin stuck her head in the freezer to cool off her thoughts, she knew that things had gone too far to turn back. She and Jonathan were traveling along a single track, each coming from opposite ends, only to merge in the center.

As soon as her hands were steady enough to carry the two tall glasses of iced tea, she returned to the living room with them. She handed Jonathan his, anticipating the energizing thrill of his touch. She was disappointed only by the fact that their contact was much too brief. Drawing in a calming breath, she moved to stand a few feet away from him, her finger absently trailing the path of condensing water as it trickled down the outside of her glass.

Jonathan watched her infinitely feminine finger and wondered how it would feel tracing him. Erin was a passionate woman—he had no doubt that she made love as fiercely as she did everything else in her life. Perhaps that was why he'd goaded her anger these past few weeks. She was gorgeous when she was in a temper. She was gorgeous anytime.

As her finger skimmed farther down the glass Jonathan imagined its delicate touch on his burning skin. A pulse jumped along his jawline, and need leapt into that part of him that was already taut and throbbing. Would she soothe his hunger or arouse his desire? Would her touch be gentle and healing or teasing and tempting? Jonathan abruptly whirled away from her until he got his thoughts, and his body, back under control.

Erin noted his move with some measure of feminine satisfaction. So she wasn't the only one prey to erotic daydreaming. She and Jonathan were in this together and they would share its inevitable apex together. Despite the heady eroticism of the moment, neither Jonathan nor Erin wanted to hurry. This trip was proving to be infinitely arousing, and they both intended to enjoy all the sights and sensual pleasures along the way.

And so they continued polishing the brass bed, knowing that each inch they cleaned brought them closer to sharing that bed. By three that afternoon Erin was almost lightheaded from the insidious seduction. For the past two hours Jonathan had been giving her slow, caressing looks that were more intoxicating than champagne. Now he'd added verbal flirtation to the campaign.

"The secret is in the polishing," he told her, as if she hadn't already noticed that. "You have to keep buffing the brass to get the most out of it." As he spoke his eyes rested on the curves beneath her shirt. He knew she wasn't wearing a bra; knew it and relished the fact that she was therefore unable to disguise what she was feeling from him.

"Stop looking at me like that," she murmured in self-defense. "Can't you read the can?" She held up the brass-polisher. "This stuff is highly inflammable. And so am I!"

"I'm counting on it."

Their polishing took on a more hurried pace after that, and they finished removing the last bit of tarnish ten minutes later.

"Done!" Erin exclaimed.

"On the contrary, we're just beginning," Jonathan countered as he tossed aside his rag. Unable to resist the temptation a second longer, he reached out to trace the vee of skin bared by her partially unbuttoned shirt. His touch not only sent Erin's senses reeling, but also it left a green mark on her skin.

The grayish-green residue of the brass tarnish had gotten off the rag and onto Jonathan's hands. He held them out for Erin's appraisal and smiled ruefully. "Is there someplace where I can clean up?"

"Sure. You can use the powder room in here." She walked over to a door near the front of the house, which Jonathan had presumed led to a coat closet.

"I'll just go clean up too. . . ." Her voice trailed away as she left Jonathan.

Erin took a very quick shower in her bathroom, using a generous application of orange blossom body soap. As soon as she'd toweled herself dry, she slipped on the silk caftan hanging on the back of her bathroom door. She emerged from the bathroom to hear Jonathan calling her name.

"Erin, do you have a bigger towel than these little things in here?"

"Sure, hang on a second." Erin grabbed a thick bath towel from the linen closet and hurried toward the powder room with it.

Jonathan was waiting for her in the living room. He'd removed his shirt and was bare from the waist up. Luckily Erin already had her arm outstretched to offer him the towel or she might well have dropped it in astonishment. She wasn't the type to swoon at the sight of a bare-chested man, but if she had been, here was one worth swooning over! A year of life-drawing class had cured whatever self-consciousness she might have had at viewing an unclothed male body, and she was usually able to admire the physical attributes of a man with all the panache of a modern, liberated woman.

But this man had the unique ability to make her feel as exhilarated as a teenager on her first date. Erin was at a loss for words, a rare state for her. She was unable to explain her overwhelming reaction. Or was she merely shying away from admitting the truth?

Rippling muscles and masculine virility were all well and good. But that wasn't the reason Erin was standing rooted to the floor as Jonathan wiped his shoulders and chest. She cared about this man, cared what he thought of her. Cared about him? Who was she kidding? She loved him.

"You okay?" Jonathan asked her. "You look like you've seen a ghost."

"I'm fine." Erin smiled because suddenly she believed that everything would be fine. Call it craziness, call it blind optimism, but Erin felt as if there were nothing she couldn't tackle.

Jonathan blinked at her glowing expression. The slinky robe Erin was wearing clung to her curves in all the right places. She'd unfastened her hair, and several dark locks fell over her forehead in a way that was very sexy.

Reading the hunger in Jonathan's eyes, Erin murmured, "We're not finished putting the bed together yet."

"Do you know if the brass headboard and footboard can

be attached to your old bed's framework?"

"All we have to do is carry the two pieces into the bedroom and they should slip right into place."

Erin didn't know if her words were intentionally provocative, but they brought to mind visions of how well she and Jonathan would fit together. She was not the only one with that mental image. Jonathan, too, was imagining himself slipping into her warm and willing haven.

Yet neither verbalized their emotions. It was too soon. Instead they concentrated their efforts on moving the headboard into the bedroom. Erin had stripped her double bed earlier in the morning, before Jonathan had even arrived.

Since Jonathan's shirt was stained with tarnish, he hadn't bothered putting it back on after he'd cleaned up. Erin was able to view the play of his muscles as he lifted his end of the heavy brass headboard. Forgotten terms from a high-school anatomy class popped back into her head. Deltoid, greater pectoral, external oblique muscles. They were all in great shape!

Erin stood propping up the headboard while Jonathan shoved the bed away from the wall. He was careful not to trap an inquisitive Butch between the bed and the trunk that served as a bedside table. The bed frame and headboard were united with little difficulty. The footboard was connected with equal ease. Jonathan had shoved the bed back against the wall before the heavy footboard was attached, so now all that was left was to make the bed.

The air was charged with anticipation as Erin brought out a stack of colorfully patterned linens in bold splashes of gold and mauve. She unfolded the bottom sheet first. The material floated over the bare mattress before it was smoothed into place by her gliding hands. Jonathan moved to the opposite side of the bed and tucked the fitted sheet in around the top and bottom corners that were nearest him.

Neither Jonathan nor Erin said a word as they made the bed. The expressions in their eyes spoke for them. If one look was worth a thousand words, then an entire illuminated manuscript was created during the installation of the bottom sheet alone.

The top sheet snapped crisply as Erin shook it out. Jonathan grabbed a top and bottom corner, working with such smooth efficiency that Erin wondered if he'd ever been in the Navy. Her father had often told her that no one could make a bed like a Navy man.

Their movements were more hurried now as they each grabbed a pillow and pulled a pillowcase over it. Both pillows hit the bed at the same time.

"You've made your bed, now you have to lie on it," Jonathan said with unmistakable desire.

"So do you," Erin returned with a sultry laugh.

Jonathan leaned across the bed and tugged her into his arms. A second later they rumpled the top sheet they'd so carefully smoothed only moments before. Jonathan rolled over so that they lay facing each other.

Erin's lips parted with breathless anticipation, but Jonathan didn't kiss them right away. Instead his kisses originated below her right earlobe. From there his lips traveled down her neck to the base of her throat where his tongue flicked across the wildly throbbing pulse point hidden there.

As if reaching a sudden decision, Jonathan eased himself slightly away from her. His eyes gazed directly into hers as he huskily murmured, "There's something I want to say."

"I've taken precautions," Erin said in a soft voice.

Jonathan shook his head. "That's not what I'm talking about."

"What, then?"

"I'm in love with you." He gently nudged her mouth closed with his finger. "There's no need to look so surprised. I'm not just saying this because I'm about to make love with you. I really mean it. I'm in love with you." When Erin didn't say a word, Jonathan prompted her to make some sort of response. "Do you believe me?"

"Yes." Erin could read the truth in his eyes, those glorious blue eyes that were no longer hidden from view by his glasses. "I believe you."

"What about you? Do you care for me?"

"Care? Jonathan, I love you. I wouldn't be with you like this if I didn't."

With a muttered groan of thankfulness Jonathan lowered his mouth to hers and kissed her passionately. It had been so long since he'd kissed her, and Jonathan fully intended to make up for all those lost hours. There was no need to reacquaint himself with the curve of her lips; their shape and taste were etched in his memory.

Erin's tongue eagerly greeted his. She moaned softly as he seduced her with tantalizing thrusts meant to symbolize their forthcoming union. His mouth engulfed hers, extracting the maximum amount of pleasure and returning it tenfold.

When his lips left hers, they moved across her face to drop soft kisses in a random pattern from her jaw to her temple. Meanwhile his hands were busy gliding the silky material off one shoulder. Erin cooperatively released Jonathan long enough to slide her arm free.

Her movement transformed the caftan into a Grecian gown that left her shoulder and arm completely bared. Jonathan celebrated the emergence of her satiny skin by running his fingertips on a caressing crusade that began at the tips of her fingers. From there he brushed over the back of her hand, slipped around to the heart of her palm, and up over her inner wrist. He paused to feel the chaotic beating of her pulse before tracing the delicate blue veins up her inner arm.

Erin lay in his arms, delighted at the tingling pleasure his touch was inciting. His fingers skimmed over the crook of her arm and continued upward to her shoulder. By the time he'd reached her collarbone, Erin was already fighting to free her other arm from the silken material. As soon as it was bared, Jonathan treated that shoulder and arm to a similar gliding exploration.

The caftan was now tenuously clinging to the slopes of her breasts. Each breath she took lowered the border between skin and silk until the material barely covered her breasts. Jonathan pulled her robe down around her waist and lowered his head. When his lips closed around one rosy tip, Erin arched upward off the bed as delicious, hot sensations shot through her. Her fingers embedded themselves in his dark hair as she held him to her.

His erotic nurturing soon had her writhing. Jonathan calmed her with his hands, soothing her even as he disposed of her caftan.

He eased away from her to devour her with his eyes. Diffuse daylight filtered onto the bed from her shaded windows and bathed her naked body in a golden glow.

"You're beautiful." His voice was hoarse, and his hand shook as he turned her face to his. He kissed her with gentle reverence.

But Erin had progressed beyond gentleness. She was impatient to explore his body as joyously as he'd explored hers. Pressing the palm of her hand against his bare shoulder, she urged him back against the bed. She then rolled over until she lay half on top of him. From this position she was able to seduce him with artful abandon.

She ran her fingertips up his muscular arm to his shoulder

and across to his collarbone. His chest was smooth and warm beneath her bare skin. She rubbed against him, delighting in the sudden raspiness of his breathing. Beneath her hand his heart kicked into overdrive. When she pressed her open mouth to him, as he'd done to her, Jonathan's entire body tightened.

He grasped her with both hands and slid her up his body until her mouth was accessible to him. Then he kissed her with a fierceness that made her shiver with excitement. Erin's hands slid down his chest to the waistband of his jeans. Her fingers were trembling as she undid the metal snap. His response was so intense that she paused, uncertain if she was pleasuring him or torturing him.

Aware of her uncertainty, Jonathan whispered words of encouragement into her ear. "Sweetheart, don't be afraid. Touch me, feel what you do to me."

He took her hand in his and guided it back down to its former resting place. Meanwhile his teeth began nibbling on her earlobe. His tongue added an electric dash of eroticism by dipping inside the sensitive opening.

Shivering beneath the sensual onslaught, Erin resumed her work on the zipper of his jeans. In a surprisingly short time his jeans joined her caftan on the floor, and seconds later his white briefs followed suit.

Now there was nothing between them, and Jonathan celebrated that fact by exploring her as intimately as she'd imagined. The reality was even better than her daydreams had been. He did indeed have magical hands, and they worked with a creative artistry that thrilled her. His evocative caresses created new dimensions of pleasure, lifting Erin from one plateau to another.

Just as she'd imagined, he found her weakest spot, rhythmically arousing her until she was rocking with pulses of joy.

Only then did he come to her. His entry was smooth and infinitely satisfying. She welcomed him, absorbing him into her very being and matching the stroking rhythm he set.

Erin's eyes widened with primitive passion as she felt the tightening promise of imminent satisfaction.

For one timeless moment she hovered on the brink before finally slipping over the edge into a warm pool of passion that left her entire being pulsating from the rippling aftershocks. Jonathan followed her soon thereafter, his body tautening and then relaxing with satiated pleasure.

Their limbs still entangled, the two lovers slipped off into a deep sleep, unaware of the white car parked a discreet distance away from Erin's gatehouse.

CHAPTER TEN

"What was that?" Erin drowsily lifted her head from Jonathan's shoulder to ask.

"My stomach."

"No, I thought I heard something." She frowned and listened intently.

"You did. My stomach." He drew her back down to him.

Erin ran the tip of her fingernail across his chest in a lazy zigzag pattern. "Are you trying to tell me something, counselor?"

"No, but my stomach is." As if confirming that fact, his stomach did indeed growl.

"So's mine," she admitted with a grin. "I'm starving." She bounced up and sent him a saucy wink over her shoulder. "Let's go raid the refrigerator."

Jonathan folded one arm beneath his head and settled himself more comfortably. "Why don't you go do that?"

"Uh-uh, this is a joint effort."

His eyes drifted shut as he heaved a contented sigh. "My joints can't make the effort."

"Wanna bet?" She slipped an impudent hand beneath the covers to launch a seductive attack on his most vulnerable front.

His eyes flew open. "Unfair interference," he decreed with a growl of pleasure.

"Why? Was I hitting below the belt?"

"You know you were."

"Any objections?"

"None at all. Do with me what you will," he invited.

Erin did and he moaned. "Why, Jonathan," she purred, "that sounds almost as if you're enjoying this."

"Whatever . . . ahhh . . . gave you . . . ummmmm . . . an idea like that?"

"Call it feminine intuition."

"I'd call it feminine sorcery," he said raspily as he reached down and captured her hand. "And unless you're willing to forego dinner and have me make a meal of you instead, you'd better stop that until after we've eaten."

"Are you ready to get up now?" she inquired playfully.

Jonathan wasn't fooled for a moment. "I would have thought the answer to that question was obvious," he drawled as he tugged her to him.

At that moment both their stomachs growled in harmony. They looked at each other and burst into laughter. Together they chanted, "Food first, fun later."

Erin played the gracious hostess by allowing Jonathan to use the bathroom first. The tactic also had the advantage of allowing her to lie back and watch him as he walked barefoot and bare-bodied from her bed to the bathroom.

"I hope I passed the audition," Jonathan declared with a roguish grin right before closing the bathroom door.

"You passed with flying colors!" Erin shouted.

She wasted several precious moments sitting in the middle of her bed with a huge grin on her face. Then the dilemma of what to wear hit her. What did one wear after making glorious, earth-shattering love in the middle of the day? Erin was certainly no expert on the matter, so she followed her instincts, which seemed to have served her pretty well so far!

After scooping up her arsenal she headed for the front powder room. The robe she wore covered her sufficiently, but she felt the need to express her emotions with an outfit that was a bit more exotic. Too bad she no longer had her belly dancing outfit; that would have suited her purposes splendidly. As it was, she made do with a delicate little creation in black silk—*little* being the operative word.

The one-piece loungewear fell somewhere in the fashion spectrum between a teddy and a romper. Thin spaghetti straps held up the chemiselike top with its lace trim and wide lacy vee neckline. Beneath the gathered elastic waistband were a pair of brief tap pants. Erin had never worn this particular little number before—she'd been waiting for a special occasion and this was it!

Erin found Jonathan in the kitchen with his head in her freezer. He wore his jeans but nothing else. "Do you know you've got a whole lobster in here?" he asked without turning around.

"I know," she purred from her sultry position against the door jamb. She had one bare foot braced against the wooden framework and one hand casually draped across her hip.

Much to her frustration, Jonathan's attention didn't waver from the freezer. "Let's eat it for dinner."

"No!" In an instant Erin had abandoned her sultry pose and raced across the kitchen to rescue the lobster. "Leave him in there. I'm going to paint him."

Jonathan's interest in the lobster vanished the moment he caught sight of Erin. His eyes slid over her with obvious relish. "Well, well, well."

Erin closed the freezer door and struck another sultry pose. "You like?"

"I like." His finger traced the lace edging as he studied her outfit with masculine appreciation. "I've never seen one of these before. What's it called?"

"Ralph."

Jonathan threw back his head and laughed. Erin found she

liked the sound of his laughter. It had a deep, rich timbre that was sexy. She also realized that he was wearing his glasses.

"You know, Mr. Garrett, now that I think about it, I rather like you with your glasses on. Maybe you should resume your stuffed-shirt image."

His face reflected his surprise. "Why?"

"Because then I'd be the only woman who knows that beneath this mild-mannered facade—"

"Mild-mannered!" Jonathan exclaimed in outrage.

". . . there lies the body and the mind of a devilish playboy. When you wear your contacts, women know you're a hunk."

"They do, huh?"

Erin nodded. "And that could be dangerous."

"For who?"

"For you," she replied, tapping an index finger against his bare chest.

Jonathan captured her finger and grinned. "You wouldn't be jealous, would you?"

"Absolutely," she readily admitted. "So be forewarned."

"Oh, I will be." He lifted her hand to his mouth and kissed each of her fingers. "But then, so should you."

"So should I what?" Her question was somewhat bemused owing to the wicked things his tongue was doing to the ultrasensitive skin between her fingers.

"Be forewarned. You're not the only one who's jealous."

She looked delightfully disbelieving. "Not you?"

"Me." He placed her hand on his heart and gazed down at her with a disapproving expression. "I've heard how busy your social life is when you're not rehearsing, Ms. Rossi. How was it put to me . . . ?" He paused to adjust his glasses authoritatively. "Oh, yes. 'Erin already has a hard time keeping track of all the men in her life,' " he quoted.

"Who told you that?"

"A good attorney never reveals his sources."

"Well, whoever it was, they exaggerated."

"Oh?"

"Yes. I've always been able to keep track of the men in my life; that's what I've got a little black book for."

"Really? And how many names are in it?"

"It's the strangest thing, actually." She leaned closer to say confidingly, "All the pages are missing except for the one marked Jonathan Garrett."

"Those pages had better stay missing," he advised her in a possessive growl.

"I'm sure they will, as long as you keep your playboy nature under wraps."

"Sounds like an equitable arrangement to me."

"I m so glad you agree with me."

"Why, Erin, I always agree with you."

"Sure, and crabs fly."

"Crabs?"

"That's what we'll be eating for dinner. Crab legs." Erin stepped away from Jonathan and headed for the kitchen cabinets above the stove, where she reached up for a large pot. "How does that sound?" she asked over her shoulder.

"Delicious." Jonathan was eyeing Erin as he drawled the word. "I've always been a leg man."

"Oh?" She placed the pot on the counter.

"Definitely." Jonathan slid his arms around her and tugged her back against him. Lowering his head, he rested his chin on the crown of her head while his hands sought out her satiny thighs. "I couldn't help but notice how gorgeous yours are. Purely my professional opinion, you understand."

"Oh, I understand." Erin leaned back and seductively rested against him.

His response was immediate. "Okay, that's it! We either

eat right now or we go back to bed hungry!"

"Where's your self-control?" she murmured.

"Not where you're looking for it," he dryly retorted as he set her away from him.

"Hey, I can control myself if you can."

"Yeah?"

"Yeah. For as long as it takes for us to eat, anyway," she qualified with a flirtatious grin. "After all, neither man nor woman doth live by love alone."

"That's true," Jonathan agreed. "Love alone is no fun. It takes two for love to work. And I do love you, Erin Rossi."

Erin's grin was transformed into a misty smile. "I love you, too, Jonathan."

"Good." He trailed the fingers of one hand down her flushed cheek. "Now that that's settled, do you think we could finally eat?"

"Certainly. In the time you make the salad, the crab will be ready."

"What salad?"

"The one you're going to create with the bibb lettuce, artichoke hearts, black olives, tomatoes, and cucumber in the refrigerator."

"Oh, that salad."

They continued exchanging quips, loving glances, and teasing touches throughout the short meal preparation.

"I've been meaning to ask you something," Jonathan said as he put the finishing garnish on the salad.

"Oh? What?"

He waved a hand at her sexy outfit. "Is this how you usually dress when you're puttering around in the kitchen?"

"Of course not," she denied in a haughty voice that was at odds with the mischievous gleam in her eyes. "Usually I wear an apron over it!"

He grinned and leered at her. "Sounds kinky."

"Oh, no. I recognize that glint in your eyes even if you are wearing glasses. Not until after we eat, remember?"

"Oh, I remember all right. Every sight, every movement, every touch . . ."

"Every growl of the stomach. Here." Erin stuck a loaded tray into Jonathan's hands and kissed his chin because that was as far as she could reach without making him bend down. "Please carry this into the dining room for me." She followed him with a bottle of wine in hand. "No, don't put it on the dining room table. We'll eat in front of the fireplace."

"Wonderful idea, except for one minor problem. You don't have a fireplace."

"Sure I do. I keep it hidden." Erin set down the wine-bottle and moved aside a hand-painted screen to reveal a small, decidedly lopsided stone fireplace located in a nook against the dining room's outside wall. "Now all we need is some sort of rug . . ."

"Bearskin?"

"Bare skin, Jonathan? I thought we agreed to wait until after we eat. Wait a second, I've got it." She raced over to a storage cabinet and rummaged around inside. "Aha!" She dragged out a rolled-up sleeping bag. "We'll use this." She closed the cabinet door and paused a moment. "Did you hear something?"

"No."

Erin made a detour over to the bay window and flipped back the sheer curtains to take a look. She saw nothing out of the ordinary outside. Shaking her head, Erin closed the window and the linen drapes in the dining room and in the living room. She also automatically checked to make sure her front door was locked.

"Now that you've doused the lights, locked the door, and

gotten out your sleeping bag, I can't wait to see what the next step is," Jonathan murmured.

"It is a bit dark in here, isn't it? Never mind, when we light the fire, it'll be much better." A fast-burning artificial log was already in the grate, so Erin only had to rip aside the paper covering and light it. "There, isn't that better?"

"Much. Now, if you'll tell me where you want me to put this tray . . ."

"Hang on, just let me spread this out. . . ." Erin untied and unzipped the sleeping bag so that she could spread it out in front of the fireplace. She then dropped to her knees and gave an inviting pat to the space next to her. "Care to join me?"

"I'd love to." Jonathan managed to do so without spilling anything on the tray he still held.

"Well done!" she said, congratulating him before giving him a kiss that quickly flared out of control.

"Any more of this fooling around and I'll be charbroiled!" he muttered against her lips. "Time out for food, remember?"

"Right."

And so they set to work, wielding a nutcracker on the hard shells of the crab legs. They ended up pulling the tender meat from the cracked crab legs with their fingers and dunking the morsels into a bowl of melted butter. The procedure left plenty of leeway for romantic elaboration as they fed each other in front of the flickering fire.

The more food they consumed, the more they were consumed by passionate desire. One thing led to another until the tray was shoved aside.

"I do believe these are getting steamed," Erin noted as she brazenly removed Jonathan's glasses and set them on the tray.

He gave her a sexy squint. "Now you're all blurry."

"Then you'll just have to come closer in order to see me better." She linked her arms around his neck.

"Excellent idea." He showed his approval by kissing his way along the silky length of her arm, all the while urging her down onto the welcoming flannel of the sleeping bag.

Erin's smile was sultry. "I thought you'd approve."

"Mmmm."

Jonathan moved against her, his leg easing its way beside hers. Erin reached up to nibble his ear while her body eagerly conformed to his. His hands slid over her, sliding the spaghetti straps from her shoulders and searching for the ultimate fastening that would free her of this bit of silk that had been driving him mad all evening.

"How do you get out of this thing?" he growled as his fingers continued their restless prowling.

"Use your imagination."

He did.

Erin was still reeling with pleasure when Jonathan carried her into the bedroom an eternity later. This time their lovemaking was furious and explosive, culminating in their simultaneous release.

The next morning brought with it the sound of steadily falling rain. Jonathan and Erin cuddled together in the brass bed and shared confidences about other rainy days in their pasts. Jonathan told Erin about his father, who was a postmaster in a small town in Connecticut, and his mother, who was a professional flutist before she'd gotten married.

"You know, there's still one thing we haven't discussed," he noted.

"What's that?"

"Our situation at Westcon."

"What about it?"

143

"We can't just leave things as they are."

"Why not?"

"Because someone is bound to find out about us." Someone most likely being Lewis Newton, Jonathan thought to himself with a frown.

"Would that be so bad?"

"It could well cost us both our jobs," Jonathan retorted. "But there is another option. You could get a job somewhere else."

Erin stiffened in his arms.

He placed a soothing hand on her shoulder. "Now keep an open mind and hear me out. We tried option one, which was obeying the corporation's rules and not seeing each other anymore. That didn't work. I love you too much to give you up. So that leaves option two: one of us is going to have to quit. And from what you've said about your job at Westcon, it makes the most sense that you be the one to leave."

Erin sat away from him to state her case. "I may not like the red tape and the regulations at Westcon, but that doesn't mean that my job is any less important to me than yours is to you. You've said that you're tired of the interoffice backbiting and power plays going on in your department. Why stay? You could get a job anywhere. Positions for graphic artists do not grow on trees, you know."

"It's true that I have little patience with the office politics, but leaving smacks too much of giving up, of surrendering, and I'm not about to do that."

"That's ridiculous!" Erin retorted with emotional vehemence. "Quitting one job for another is not giving up or surrendering. People change jobs all the time. And if you're going to argue on the basis of seniority, I've worked for Westcon longer than you have."

"Erin, I've told you, I'm up for a big promotion. I'll admit that I have gotten several offers from other companies, but none of them match the challenge and responsibility that I would have at Westcon."

His explanation in no way appeased Erin's anger. In fact, it only served to ignite it further. "So what you're telling me is that I have to give up my job so you can sit back in your cushy job?"

"No!" Now it was Jonathan's turn to display his temper. "My job is no cushier than yours is."

"Come on." Erin angrily got out of bed and pulled on her robe. "You've got a fifth-floor office in the Ivory Tower while I'm sitting behind a drafting table in the West Tower with all the other workers."

"What does the location of our offices have to do with anything?" His question was laced with equal parts of irritation and impatience.

The combination proved to have a combustible impact on Erin's temper. "That's why you automatically assumed that I should be the one to quit. After all, I'm only a menial worker and you're a professional, right?" Her voice had risen to a yell.

"Quit putting words into my mouth!" Jonathan shouted before shoving back the covers and grabbing his clothing. He was dressed in record time. "You're obviously in no state to discuss the matter rationally." He shoved the case for his contacts into his shirt pocket.

"Sure." She immediately followed him when he stormed off into the living room in search of his glasses. "Blame it all on the emotional woman!"

"You said it, not me." Having found his glasses, Jonathan put them on, unlocked the front door, and yanked it open.

Erin was seething. "Don't you dare walk out in the middle of a fight!"

While Erin and Jonathan were glaring at each other on the threshold of Erin's front door, Lewis Newton was hurriedly aiming his camera at them and focusing it. The leaves of the bush he was hiding behind across the street partially blocked his shot, so he moved slightly to his left. Perfect. Now he could see everything. Jonathan's shirt wasn't buttoned and Erin's robe was slipping off one shoulder. Lewis saw it all very clearly through his telephoto lens as he rapidly snapped away picture after picture. He couldn't have hoped for a more incriminating series of shots, Lewis thought to himself with glee as he kept snapping until Jonathan had gotten into his car and driven away. This should wrap up his case against Jonathan once and for all.

CHAPTER ELEVEN

Erin felt hollow inside. Jonathan had left an hour ago. She'd been sitting on the window seat, crying, ever since then. A few minutes ago Butch had jumped up to offer his condolences. She'd gathered the tomcat into her arms and cried into his soft fur. Butch had graciously allowed himself to be used as a security blanket.

"How did things go so wrong so quickly?" Erin's question to the cat was voiced on the tail end of a hiccup.

Butch shook his head and jumped down to give chase to a fly.

Erin attempted to wipe away her tears with the back of her hand. How had things gotten so complicated? Who said the road to true love had to be this rocky?

But was it true love? Or only a close facsimile? Erin didn't doubt her feelings for Jonathan, but she did question the depth of his feelings for her. He'd said he loved her, but not until they'd been on the verge of making love. And while she knew he'd meant the words at the time, she wasn't sure how much the declaration had been affected by the passion of the moment.

And yet she hadn't realized the full depth of her feelings for him until yesterday, either. Or, more accurately speaking, she hadn't admitted those feelings, even to herself, until then. What a mess! Erin wiped a weary hand across her eyes. She couldn't think straight anymore. They'd been so happy last night. Then reality had returned this morning and thrown everything into a chaotic mess.

Erin's anger had long since drained away, leaving behind a sediment of pain. Jonathan claimed he loved her, but when it had come down to the crunch, he'd chosen Westcon over her. He hadn't taken her feelings into consideration at all. And he'd never mentioned the future and whether he'd wanted her to share his.

For all his talk of love there had been no words of commitment. Erin knew the two didn't always go together in today's world where casual relationships were used as a means of avoiding permanency. She also knew that she wanted more out of life. She might be bohemian about some things, but when it came to love, she shared a lot of the old-fashioned ideals of her parents.

Regardless of her own personal trauma, there was still a play to put on, and the final technical runthrough was only a few hours away. Erin busied herself with cleaning the gatehouse—removing the dishes from in front of the fireplace and returning the screen to its former position. She stripped the bed and stuffed the linens into the bottom of her dirty clothes hamper. All the while memories kept threatening to overwhelm her, but Erin did her best to keep them at bay.

Knowing she'd be doing a lot of running and rummaging at the theater, Erin wore a pair of sweatpants in regulation gray and a cherry-red sweatshirt. The theater was already crowded when she arrived.

"There are still tickets available for next Monday night's performance," Lilli Martin, the director of ticket sales, was telling the people working on the stage setting. "Friday, Saturday, and Sunday nights are sold out. If anyone wants more information, have them call me."

Tickets, as such, were not printed for the performances. Instead the director of ticket sales for each production made a list of people's names, much as a maître d' would do at a fine restaurant. When people arrived at the theater, Lilli would greet them and ask for their names. Then she'd tick them off her master list and have one of the members of her committee show them to their seats. The seats were not reserved and were usually filled on a first-come first-served basis. At the present time the theater seated seventy people.

Erin was glad not to have to worry about the so-called house end of the production. The house was that area of the theater in which the audience was seated, and Erin knew that Lilli was more than capable of handling the job. Besides, supervising Lilli was Dan's job as producer.

Dan arrived at the theater shortly after Erin did, looking rather wan but claiming that he felt better. Martha got him a cup of chamomile tea and generally fussed over him until he retreated to the prop room for some peace and quiet.

Up in the sound-and-light booth, Ned was practicing dimming the houselights and trying to fix some malfunctioning switch that made two stubborn lights remain lit when all the others went out.

Erin welcomed all the commotion, for it kept her mind off other things—namely Jonathan. A part of her dreaded seeing him while another part couldn't wait. But both parts agreed on one thing: the other members of the Village Players had all worked too hard for anyone's personal problems to interfere with the production at this late date. Everyone had put in hours of time and labor to get this show ready, and Erin wasn't about to sabotage their efforts. Somehow she knew Jonathan would feel the same way.

It wasn't as difficult as either of them had anticipated. Now that all the scenery was on stage, including doors that really opened and closed, furniture and props that really existed; and now that all the actors wore their costumes and knew their blocking and their lines, the play had taken on a reality, a life of its own.

For that brief period of time Paul became Algernon Moncrieff; Sue, Gwendolen Fairfax, and even Jonathan truly became John Worthing—alias Ernest. Such was the magic of the theater.

The play was performed without interruption, as it had been for the past week. Erin had learned that running the show without a break increased the actors' feel for the flow and timing of the production. Any late entrances or missed cues could be pointed out at the end of the play. That afternoon everything went perfectly, right on schedule. No one missed any lines, the stage crew changed the set in record time without losing any props, and the sound effects came in right on cue.

When it was all over, everyone shared a sigh of relief and smiles of congratulation. Then they all headed for the Lion's Inn Pub. Everyone except for Jonathan and Erin, both of whom went home alone—Jonathan to think things through and Erin to cry herself to sleep.

There was no rehearsal scheduled Monday. The next rehearsals would be Tuesday's and Wednesday's full-scale dress rehearsals complete with a small audience of senior citizens from a nearby retirement home. Thursday would be a final day of rest before the play opened Friday night for its week-long run.

On Monday Erin had a hard time keeping her mind on her work. Across the way, in his fifth-floor office in the executive East Tower, Jonathan was suffering from the same problem. A few doors away Lewis Newton was also merely rearranging his papers instead of completing any real work as he impatiently awaited his four-thirty appointment with Mr. Rahmsbottom. Lewis had tried to get in to see Mr. R. earlier, but that she-dragon, Mrs. Bunt, had firmly informed him that her boss was tied up with appointments until then.

Consequently Lewis had to cool his heels all day waiting for his big moment. By the time it came, he'd rehearsed his lines as well as any actor.

Lewis began by asking, "Do you remember that matter we discussed several weeks ago, sir?"

Mr. R. didn't look up from the report he was studying. "What matter was that, Newton?"

"It concerned Jonathan Garrett and his possible involvement with a female employee here at Westcon in violation of personnel regulations."

"Get to the point," Mr. R. ordered impatiently. "I haven't got all day."

"The point is that Jonathan has continued his liaison with this woman from the graphic arts department."

Mr. R. looked up, his piercing gaze pinning the younger attorney. "On what basis are you making that claim?"

"On the basis of these pictures." Lewis handed the eight-by-ten enlargements to Mr. R.

"This woman"—Mr. R. pointed at Erin's picture—"she's the one from the graphic arts department?"

"She's the one. Her name is Erin Rossi, sir, and she's been working for Westcon for three years now. I've got a copy of her personnel file here for you, should you be interested."

"Good work, Newton." Mr. R. took the file. "I appreciate your bringing this to me. You know, Westcon always rewards corporate loyalty."

"That's not why I brought it to your attention," Lewis lied. "I just didn't like the fact that Jonathan was carrying on behind your back this way. It reflects badly on all of us here in Legal. As attorneys we owe it to our profession to obey the regulations that are drawn up. If we have some argument about their legality, then we should confront the issue, not try to skulk around it."

"I agree, Lewis."

Lewis fairly beamed. It was the first time Mr. R. had ever called him by his first name. "I'm glad you feel that way, sir."

"I think you're going to go far with this corporation, Lewis. You've got the right attitude. I like that in a man!"

"Why, thank you, sir."

Mr. R. got up from his chair and came around the desk to place an avuncular arm around Lewis's shoulders as he escorted the younger man toward the office door. "You leave this matter to me, Lewis. I'll handle it personally."

Lewis was not thrilled to hear that. He longed to ask how and when Jonathan would be reprimanded, but he knew to do so would be pushing his luck. So he had to bow to Mr. R.'s decision and hope for the best.

The moment Mr. R. returned to his desk, he pressed the intercom button to his secretary's desk and barked into the phone. "Get me the head of personnel at once!"

While he was waiting for the call to be put through, Mr. Archibald Rahmsbottom glared at Erin's photograph and sorted through her personnel file. He had no intention of allowing some wanton woman to ruin the plans he'd so carefully laid out for Jonathan.

Erin had arranged to take Tuesday and Wednesday off work as vacation days because of the dress rehearsals, and as she headed down to the Little Theatre early Tuesday morning, she was glad she had. Invariably there were a thousand and one little details to take care of before the dress rehearsal, and since Dan still wasn't feeling quite up to par, Erin had volunteered to help organize things in whatever way she could.

She'd brought along some clippings from the local newspapers to add to the scrapbook of the production's progress. The articles featured pictures of the group rehearsing while in costume. Despite the grainy quality of the newspaper photos, Jonathan still looked wonderful. So did all the players, Erin silently added, purposely removing her attention from Jonathan.

For the moment Erin was still sticking by her I'll-think-about-things-later routine. Preparations for the play kept her so busy that she skipped lunch. Pre-performance nerves were responsible for her skipping dinner.

In just a few hours her production would be performed for the first time before an audience. Even though it was only a dress rehearsal and the audience hadn't paid to get in, to be effective everything had to be played as if it were the real thing. The players all arrived early, eager to get things started. One by one they trooped downstairs into the care of the members of the costume and makeup committees until their cue was called.

The Little Theatre lacked anything as grand as separate dressing rooms. Instead, most of the basement area had been turned into a communal dressing area. Lighted mirrors lined one wall with a long shelf beneath it for all the assorted greasepaints, liners, hair dryers and other accoutrements needed for creating the characters appearance.

The "techies," those involved with the technical aspect of the production, as opposed to the "hams," who performed on stage, were out in full force. Ned and his assistant were standing on stepladders, making final adjustments to the lights. Prop girls were busily making sandwiches for the tea tray in Act One. The florist finally delivered the rosebushes everyone had been waiting for, and Erin's supervision was needed in their proper placement for Act Two. Bells and other assorted noises filled the air as another of Ned's assistants tested the sound-effects equipment.

Wanda was backstage, sitting at a small table with the prompt book laid open before her and a lightweight headset on her head. The intercom audio system was hooked up to both the sound-and-light booth and the basement dressing room area. This way Wanda could notify everyone of their cues.

Erin sat out front, determined not to show her nervousness. She was the leader of the troops, someone meant to inspire confidence, and she played her role perfectly. Unfortunately the dress rehearsal didn't go perfectly.

It began with someone—they never identified who—whistling in the dressing room, an omen of bad luck among superstitious theater people. Sure enough, Roger, who was playing Merriman the butler, almost tripped over a loose corner of the carpet in Act Two. His recovery was excellent, but it threw Cindy off-stride a bit.

Things got worse during the second intermission. First one piece of furniture was missing, so the interval lasted twenty minutes (until the chair was found) instead of the usual twelve. The leather bag that solved the mystery of John Worthing's true identity as Ernest also disappeared. A frantic search ensued before it was located, behind a potted plant backstage.

To top it all off there was a problem with the sound effects in Act Three. Martha, as Lady Bracknell said, "This noise is extremely unpleasant" to utter silence instead of a recorded racket. Artie stepped into the breach by ad-libbing, "It's quiet now," before continuing with his normal line.

The audience didn't even notice the small lapses and clapped enthusiastically when the play was completed. Their applause made all the work worthwhile.

Wednesday's dress rehearsal went more smoothly, thanks in part to Erin's assurances the previous night that "A bad dress rehearsal means a good opening night." The theatrical cliché loosened the players' fears and encouraged them to keep reaching for that perfect performance. Again the presence of a small but enthusiastic audience improved the actors' self-confidence about appearing in front of a crowd.

Thursday Erin returned to work to find an interoffice envelope sitting in the middle of her drawing table. It was marked CONFIDENTIAL AND URGENT. Something told her it did not contain good news. Even with that premonition in mind, Erin was still stunned by the letter's contents.

It was typed on Westcon letterhead and was signed by the head of the personnel department.

Dear Ms. Rossi:

It has come to our attention that you have been in serious violation of Article IV section 4.19 of Westcon's Personnel Policy concerning nepotism and dating between Westcon employees. Please note that when you signed your original employment contract with Westcon, you agreed to comply with all the bylaws and regulations contained within the Personnel Policy Handbook. A hearing concerning this complaint against you is scheduled for October 1, at which time the matter of your termination will be decided.

Sincerely yours,
Graham Johnson
Head of Personnel.

The letter fell from Erin's hands and fluttered back to her drawing table. At that moment her boss walked into her cubbyhole.

"Hey, welcome back. How's the play going? The wife and

I have reservations for Saturday night, you know." Carl Mather paused as he realized that Erin obviously was not herself. "Is something wrong, Erin?"

"You could say that," she replied in a bitter voice. She handed him the letter.

Carl read it and muttered, "I'll be damned!"

"No, it looks like *I* will be and by the full tribunal of the Personnel Review Board, no less!"

"What are you going to do?" Carl asked her.

"Mover and shaker that I am, you mean?" Erin's voice was uneven.

Carl did not see any connection between his question and her reply. That fact worried him. "Stay calm, Erin. Don't panic."

"I'm not going off the deep end, Carl," Erin reassured him. "Not yet, anyway. I'd just like to know how this thing got started."

"Article IV, section 4.19," Carl reread. "I'd have to look that up in the P.P. Handbook to see what it refers to."

"I'll save you the trouble. They're referring to my involvement with a Westcon employee. Someone in the legal department. We met outside of work, and I didn't realize he was employed here until . . ."

"It was too late," Carl tactfully supplied.

"I want to know how the Personnel Department found out about it. Do you think you could help me do that, Carl?"

"I'll see what I can do," he promised.

Carl got back to her half an hour later. "My sources tell me that the complaint originated from the legal department."

The legal department? For one brief distraught moment the possibility crossed her mind that Jonathan might have something to do with this action against her. But then common sense prevailed. Jonathan would only be implicating himself by instigating such a claim. In one thing he had already proved himself to be utterly consistent, and that was in his dedication to his job. He wouldn't knowingly do anything to jeopardize that. But if a complaint had been filed against her, it stood to reason that a similar complaint may well have been filed against Jonathan. Which would mean that he could be in danger of losing his job because of her.

"Did your contact in the personnel department say if anyone else had been served with a letter like the one I received?" Erin asked Carl.

"No, they didn't say. All they told me was that the action had originated from the legal department, from the top man himself, it seems. Where are you going?" Carl called after Erin as she marched out of her office.

"To the Ivory Tower," she replied, her jaw set and ready for battle. "To see the top man in Legal."

When she arrived at the fifth floor offices of the legal department, Erin was greeted by a pleasant secretary.

"Who's in charge of this department?" Erin rapped out the question with unmistakable authority.

"Mr. Rahmsbottom."

"Where's his office?"

"At the end of the hall, but I'm afraid . . ."

"No need for you to be afraid, it's Mr. Rahmsbottom who'd better look out," Erin muttered as she turned on her heel and marched down the hallway.

In all her years of acting as Mr. R.'s secretary, Mrs. Bunt had never allowed anyone to get past her without an appointment. But then, she'd never come across anyone as determined as Erin before.

"Is Mr. Rahmsbottom in?"

Erin could tell just by looking at the secretary's face that he was. Mrs. Bunt didn't say a word; she was too stunned at

157

the young woman breathing fire on the other side of her desk.

A moment later Erin had sailed past her and entered the inner domain of Archibald Rahmsbottom—without being announced.

Mrs. Bunt was horrified. She scurried after Erin. "You can't come in here—"

"I'm already in here," Erin pointed out from her position a few inches in front of Mr. Rahmsbottom's desk.

"Shall I call Security, sir?" Mrs. Bunt asked Mr. R.

"My name is Erin Rossi, Mr. Rahmsbottom," Erin regally announced. "I think you and I need to have a little talk." Her eyes were fiery with determination.

But Mr. R. had already recognized Erin from the photographs he'd seen of her. "That's all right, Mrs. Bunt." He waved his secretary away. "I'll handle this. You can go back to your desk now."

Mrs. Bunt was reluctant to leave her boss unprotected. "Are you sure, sir?"

"I'm positive. That will be all, Mrs. Bunt."

Erin was about to launch into her tirade when her attention was captured by a pile of photographs strewn across one corner of Mr. Rahmsbottom's huge desk. They were pictures of herself and Jonathan as he was leaving her gatehouse Sunday morning. Here was her answer to how they'd been found out. Someone had been spying on them!

Erin grabbed hold of the pictures and exclaimed, "This is sick! It's a blatant invasion of privacy, and if it's not illegal, then it should be! And your being an attorney makes it even worse. Or did you only study the law in order to learn how to circumvent it?" Erin was not pulling her punches. "What did you do, order one of your lackeys to follow Jonathan and me around?"

"I didn't order anyone, Ms. Rossi," Mr. Rahmsbottom

calmly denied. He appeared unscathed by her fiery denunciation. "These photographs were given to me by someone who was concerned about the breach in professional behavior between yourself and one of my best attorneys."

"So you instigated a witch-hunt against us? If Jonathan is one of your best attorneys, then why are you doing this to him? Don't you realize what a complaint like this could do to his career?" Erin demanded.

"I realize that very well, probably better than you do, Ms. Rossi. That's why it was decided that you should be the one to leave Westcon, not Jonathan. Someone of his caliber is not easily replaceable. You are."

"I see." Erin had one more question she had to ask.

"Does Jonathan know about all of this?"

"Yes, he knows."

"I see," she repeated dully.

Erin had left the office before Mr. R. could say another word.

"What was that all about?" Mrs. Bunt inquired as she came in moments later with a stack of correspondence for Mr. R. to sign.

"She came here to defend Jonathan Garrett against losing his job," Mr. R. replied, although he didn't think insulting either attorneys or himself was a very good way to go about that.

"But Jonathan Garrett resigned this morning, Mr. R."

"I know that, Mrs. Bunt, but apparently Ms. Rossi doesn't."

Erin returned to her office and began systematically clearing out her things from her cubbyhole. In fifteen minutes she'd gathered the few personal effects she'd kept in the office. Westcon had always frowned upon its employees keeping mementos in their work space.

"What are you doing?" Carl asked in a horrified voice when he stopped by to see how Erin was faring.

"I'm leaving. I'm not going to give Westcon the satisfaction of discussing my termination. They can't fire me, because I quit!"

"Erin, don't you want to think about this before you do anything drastic?"

"No."

Erin was too upset to go home. She drove around the city for a while and somehow ended up at Kelley Point Park without any clear recollection of how she got there. The day was cloudy and cool, but Erin paid no attention to the weather. Instead she took the path that led down to the river, and sat along its banks. Perhaps she should have been a tugboat captain after all.

Erin had no idea how long she sat there, aimlessly staring at the river and clearing her mind of all thought. When a damp drizzle began to fall, blocking her view of the river traffic, she got to her feet and returned to her Voyager, much wetter than when she'd set out.

"You look like a drowned rat!" Mary exclaimed when Erin showed up at her house. "What happened? Why aren't you at work?"

"I quit." Those were the only two words Erin could get out before she started crying silent, continuous tears that tore at Mary's heart.

Mary insisted that Erin stay the night. Erin was too tired to argue. There was no real need for her to go home. Butch had enough dry cat food left out in his dish that he wouldn't go hungry. She stayed, glad to be away from the gatehouse with its painful memories of the night she and Jonathan had made love. She put off going back home until late the next afternoon, and then she only stayed long enough to feed Butch, take a shower, and change. Her black dress with its brilliant blue belt matched her feelings. Erin felt black and blue inside.

Returning to the theater that evening was one of the hardest things Erin had ever been called upon to do. But as soon as opening night was over, she'd be turning the play over to Wanda. When the curtain went up, the director's job was over. Then it was up to the stage manager to run the show. And maybe then Erin could forget that Jonathan Garrett had ever walked into her parents' dry cleaners in search of his trousers. Maybe then she could forget that she'd offered to teach the supposed stuffed shirt how to relax and have a good time. Maybe then she could forget she'd ever fallen in love with him. Maybe; but Erin knew that that time would be a long time coming.

A quiet, almost threatening feeling hit Erin the moment she walked into the theater. She told herself it was because of opening night. There was always a hushed silence backstage on opening night, the usual hustle-bustle having been replaced by a tense seriousness as everyone realized that this was it. Erin was prepared for that. But as was often the case, she was not prepared for Jonathan.

"Where the hell have you been?"

Before she could reply to his ragged question, he'd hooked his arm around her waist and hauled her against him. Only then did she realize that Jonathan was trembling. He buried his face in her hair, blind to the curious looks he was getting from the stage hands.

"I waited outside your house all night, and you never came home. I was worried sick about you." He reluctantly loosened his hold on her. "Don't you ever do that to me again."

His husky order restored Erin's voice. "Me do that to you? What about what you've done to me?"

Cathie Linz

"Come on, we've got to talk." He tugged her after him in search of some quiet privacy. There was no such thing upstairs; even the prop room was crowded.

"But you're not even in your costume yet," she exclaimed as he pulled her downstairs.

"There's plenty of time." He opened the door marked FURNACE ROOM and tugged her inside before closing the door.

Familiar with her surroundings, Erin reached out to flick on the light. "Are you crazy? You've got a play to perform in less than"—she studied her watch—"an hour from now."

"You don't have to worry," he assured her. "I'm not going to let them get away with this."

Was he suffering from acute stage fright or what?

"Get away with what?"

"Firing you. I know all about your hearing in front of the Personnel Review Board on October first. And I want you to know that you're not going to have to face it alone. I'll be your legal counsel."

"But, Jonathan . . ."

"I know it's not my field of expertise, but I've called a friend from the American Civil Liberties Union, and he's agreed to help me research the cites and legal precedents."

Erin had a hard time assimilating what he was saying. "Let me get this straight. You're telling me that you want to defend me at my hearing?"

"That's right."

"Why?"

"Because I love you."

For her own protection Erin refused to let herself be swayed by his words. He'd hurt her so much already, she couldn't cope with another misunderstanding. "What about Westcon?" she inquired with some degree of bitterness. "I'm sure they're not going to appreciate one of their own attorneys defending me."

"I don't work for Westcon any longer," he quietly informed her.

Erin was shocked. "What?"

"I quit yesterday morning. As soon as I was told about your hearing, as a matter of fact. That's when I decided that I didn't want to continue working for a corporation that demanded such blind obedience." Jonathan saw no point in upsetting Erin with the details of how they'd been spied upon or a description of his confrontation with Lewis Newton. One thing was certain: the jerk would never use that camera again! "But I don't want you losing your job because of me. We'll fight this thing clear to the U.S. Supreme Court if we have to."

"Jonathan, that's not necessary. I quit yesterday too."

"You mean . . ."

". . . that we're both unemployed. Yes, it does look that way."

"I don't believe this."

"Neither do I," she admitted. "I thought you approved of Westcon's action against me."

"Whatever gave you that idea?"

"When I went to talk to your boss, Mr. Sheepsbottom, or whatever his name was—"

"Wait a second," Jonathan said, interrupting her. "You went to talk to Mr. Rahmsbottom? What for?"

"To save your job."

"My job? I don't understand."

"I thought you must have gotten the same notice that I did," Erin explained. "I didn't want you losing your job and your promotion because of me."

"So you went to see Mr. Rahmsbottom?"

"That's right. And the man had photographs of us on his desk! The pervert!"

Jonathan almost choked at Erin's description of his staid and ultraconservative ex-boss.

"I told him exactly what I thought of him, and then I asked him not to ruin your career by pressing a complaint against you. That's when he told me that I was the one who would be leaving Westcon, not you. And he said that you were aware of the plan. He didn't say anything about you quitting."

Jonathan swore under his breath. "So you thought I'd gone along with his little plan to get rid of you."

Erin nodded.

"Hey, you two, we've got a play to put on out here!" The shout was accompanied by a two-fisted knock on the door.

"Be right out," Jonathan promised. "Just know that I love you, Erin," he murmured before dropping a passionate kiss on her parted lips. "We'll work out the rest after the play."

There was no more time to talk after that as the preparations for the play went into their final stages. Jonathan was hurried into his costume and worked over by the makeup people. Erin purposefully stayed away, because otherwise she knew she'd be tempted to grab hold of him and kiss him as passionately as he'd kissed her!

Everyone was making last-minute checks, both actual and mental, confirming that they'd done their part in making sure the performance would run smoothly. All of them—actors, stagehands, wardrobe people, sound-and-light crew—were listening to the tension-building countdown. "Half hour . . . fifteen minutes." At that point Erin went downstairs to give the players all a brief pep talk, and then she went out into the audience. The house was full. Erin's thoughts remained backstage where she knew Wanda would be continuing the countdown: "Five minutes," "Places on stage, please," and then, "Lights!"

The spotlights went on, and the play began. Paul spoke, his voice strong and confident. Jonathan entered and crossed to the love seat, that infamous love seat from Mrs. Durkee's attic. Erin's smile became misty, and her cheeks flushed as her thoughts veered away from the play onto more intimate recollections. The sound of the audience's laughter brought her back to the play's action. The reviews would later read that "The Village Players' production of *The Importance of Being Earnest* proved a worthwhile showcase; not only for Oscar Wilde's witty dialogue and ingenious plot but also for the talented cast of actors who performed their parts with a perfect sense of timing. Bravo!"

The performance was followed by nonstop applause and cheers as everyone took their bows, including Erin, who was applauded by the cast and crew as well as the audience. Five minutes later the downstairs dressing room had been transformed into a celebratory circus. Well-wishers and family members came down to congratulate the actors. Other members of the Village Players offered their support and heartfelt praise.

Erin searched the crowd for Jonathan. She finally found him surrounded by people who were shaking his hand and slapping him on the shoulder. That was all well and good, but the eager line of women kissing him was another matter entirely!

Excusing herself from her own group of well-wishers, Erin resolutely made her way through the crowd to Jonathan's side. "Excuse us a moment, won't you? I need to confer with Jonathan privately."

Jonathan grinned down at her and whispered, "Where to? The furnace room again?"

Erin nodded.

A few moments later they were locked in the relatively quiet confines of the furnace room with the muted noise of the crowd outside and the clanking noise of the hot-water heater inside.

Jonathan hadn't had the time even to remove his makeup, let alone his costume. Erin didn't care. She couldn't wait a second later to kiss him and tell him how much she loved him.

"Even if I am unemployed?" he murmured against her mouth.

"Even then."

Jonathan loosened his hold on her so that he could gaze down into her face. "That's nice to know. However, I won't be unemployed for long. I've decided to accept an offer from the BMI Corporation. Their headhunter's been after me for some time now."

"I know the feeling," Erin murmured with a seductive laugh. She slid her arms around his waist and beneath his nineteenth-century suit jacket. Leaning against him, she allowed the tips of her breasts to taunt the broad planes of his chest. "I've been after you for some time myself."

"Mmm," he groaned as approval of her seductive movement. "You've got me. How about making it permanent and legal?"

"Is that a proposal?"

"Yes." His hands dipped to the small of her back where he caressed her with possessive intimacy.

Erin melted against him. "I'm glad. Because I'd love to make things permanent and legal with you, Mr. Garrett, now that you've learned the importance of being earnest!"

Jonathan's mouth stole the laughter from her lips as his hand played over her, urging her to him. There was tenderness as well as passion in his embrace, need as well as desire. Shivering with pleasure, Erin expressed her love through the richness of her response. Jonathan had just begun to explore the swell of her breast when once again their embrace was interrupted by someone banging on the door.

"Hey, you two, we're all going over to Dan's for the cast party. Are you coming or not?"

"We're having our own party in here," Jonathan informed them. "You all go on ahead. We'll catch up with you."

"Later," Erin added.

"Much later," Jonathan agreed before kissing her again.